Teal's Gold

In the bed of a remote New Mexico creek, Austin Teal strikes gold. But when the old placer miner gets shot dead in a Calido Run gunfight, he's only managed to disclose a few cryptic words about its exact location to his young son.

Five years on, Wesley Teal sets out to solve the riddle, tracking down the source of his pa's gold. But he's been watched and trailed. Unscrupulous hardcases follow him; men like Grover Garve who will stop at nothing where the prospect of a golden fortune is concerned. So, with the help of Amy Chard, Wes has to fight them off, first in the bars and streets, then out across the gruelling terrain.

Teal's Gold

Abe Dancer

A Black Horse Western

ROBERT HALE · LONDON

ISBN 978-0-7090-9964-2

Robert Hale Limited
Clerkenwell House
Clerkenwell Green
London EC1R 0HT

www.halebooks.com

Typeset by
Derek Doyle & Associates, Shaw Heath
Printed and bound in Great Britain by
CPI Antony Rowe, Chippenham and Eastbourne

1

Poke Lemmer shuffled his backside in the tub chair, lifted his feet to the puncheon trestle that served as office space at the rear of the livery. 'You got me a yarn, Wes . . . some sort o' windy?' he asked, twisting his fingers through the long curls of his beard.

Wesley Teal shrugged his shoulders into his jacket, and shook his head. 'No. But maybe I'm working on something,' he replied casually.

Lemmer sniffed, then smiled. He'd almost given up hope of getting any sort of conversation from this young man. Wesley Teal acted like talk was stock – a secure investment in the town's bank. In the few months he'd been working at the livery, he'd rarely offered up more than a sentence. Consequently, no one in Mariposa knew much about him, except that he was no greenhorn, and very good with horses.

Tittle-tattle formed the most interesting part of

Lemmer's daily routine, but his wily questioning had gleaned next to nothing about Wesley's past and private life. At first, he'd figured that Wesley was a young drifter, then wondered if he was a sufferer who'd been sent to a dry climate for the betterment of his health. Wesley was more than six feet tall, and pared down to bone and muscle, but to Lemmer's eye he was of sickly countenance in spite of the vigorous way he worked. Another thing that irked Lemmer was the way Wesley visited the saloon for a glass of beer, but didn't trade more than a couple of words with anyone. Then he'd go on to Bernardo's Beans for his supper before returning to his lodging over the livery. And it was always at the same time each and every evening.

'I'll be off now. Goodnight,' Wesley offered, as if sensing Lemmer's thoughts.

'Headed for Sappers,' Lemmer said. The unnecessary question had become routine, an alternative response. 'Maybe one night you should stay awhile . . . get yourself distracted. You ever storm any puncheons, son?' he went on, hoping for an outcome.

'No. Not that I recall.'

'Well you don't know what you're missin'.' Lemmer heaved himself from his chair, lumbered into a tight circle, flapping his arms, stamping a foot and cackling. Then he sat down again and puffed out his cheeks. 'There was a time when I could hoof with the best of 'em,' he rasped. 'It's more'n wrigglin' round an' shakin' your rump. But I'll wager them dancin' girls are real appreciative of a young feller like you, Wes.'

'I'm not interested.'

'Wherever it was you come from, weren't there any entertainin' for young bucks? No offence, son, but you ain't one o' them heifer brands, are you?'

A hard, but fleeting ghost of a smile, crossed Wesley's face. 'No,' he said, economically.

'Then what the hell's wrong with you?' Lemmer muttered, irritated by Wesley's reserve. 'It just ain't natural. Go get yourself some livin',' he added.

The tough smile came back to Wesley's face as he ambled along the boardwalk towards the bright, lantern-lit front of Sappers Hole saloon. Lemmer's questions had amused him in a dour way, and he wondered how long it would be before the old feller's curiosity really got the better of him.

Wesley shouldered his way through the batwings into the low-hanging smoke, grimacing at the pungent tang of cowboy, tobacco and liquor. He went across to where the bar cornered into the back wall, away from the groups congregated out front. The barkeep didn't have to ask him what he wanted, just nod his recognition, fill a long glass and slide it across the wet-topped counter.

Wesley looked at the frothy head of beer and slid a coin back in return. He couldn't afford more than one drink. *Not for a while*, he thought as he lifted the glass.

Ten minutes later, he'd got to thinking about his bowl of chili stew when the near sound of a voice made him flinch. His already sallow skin drained of more colour and he tightened his fingers around the glass, but didn't turn his head.

He recalled the cold, flat voice as though he'd heard it only yesterday. It had stuck in his mind, along with the dark-featured face with its twisted beak of a nose.

Wesley finished his beer in one pull. There would be no appreciative spinning-out this evening. The sound of the man's voice had suddenly taken care of that.

He set down the glass and edged away from the bar. Only when he was well clear, did he turn for a discreet look back. There were a few drinkers standing in between, but he had a profile view that confirmed the man was Farley Korne. Two men stood alongside Korne; a big Apache half-breed with scarred cheeks, and a shorter thickset man with wintry, pale eyes. Although it had been five years since their last meeting, seeing the three of them again brought back vivid memories to Wesley, and his heart started to thump heavily.

This is no coincidence, he thought, and cursed. *Yeah, that's it. They've been waiting in Calido Run for a few goddamn months, and now they've trailed me here.*

The hawk-featured Korne said something to the barkeep, and Wesley saw the man look towards the corner where he'd just been standing. Then the barkeep looked around the room, beyond the group at the bar, then directly at him. Wesley chewed on another damning curse as he turned for the batwings, but he was too late.

'Hey, Wes . . . Wes Teal,' the barkeep called out. 'Feller here askin' for you.'

Wesley flicked a glance towards the batwings, but headlong flight wasn't in his nature or the sharp answer, even. He turned around slowly, flexing the fingers of both hands.

Korne's tight mouth was pulled into a grin, his dark eyes gleaming as he took a step forward. 'Howdy Wes, I hope you weren't leavin' on my account,' he said. 'I've been lookin' for you. We've got unfinished business.'

Wesley shook his head, coolly. 'We don't have any-thing, Korne,' he answered.

'No, you're wrong, boy,' Korne corrected. 'Have you forgotten the deal between Caleb Dawes an' your pa?'

When Korne's two sidekicks stepped away from the bar, a nerve worked in Wesley's jaw. He took a breath and moved a pace nearer the three men. 'They're both dead.'

'Yeah, but the deal ain't,' Korne said. 'You took over your pa's share, an' we took over Dawes's. You recall these friends o' mine, Jack Bass an' Mose Parker?' he added. 'They're part o' the business.'

'I recall them. They were there the night my pa was murdered,' Wesley replied. His voice was low and threatening, cutting through the stillness that had suddenly befallen the saloon. Not one of its customers knew what the confrontation was about, but they all recognized the antagonism, the rising tension. Now at last, perhaps they would learn something about the quiet, young hostler.

'Your pa was killed in self-defence,' Korne responded brusquely, closing in and beginning to crowd Wesley. 'That's what the law said, an' it was the same law that did right by you, Wes. You know it, an' despite what you think, we ain't finished.'

'Well, I say we are,' Wesley said. 'Finished for good.'

'It ain't a decision that suits me, Wes. We'll get ourselves a table an' talk it through civil like. A sort o' shareholders' meetin'.'

'I've got me a meeting somewhere else, Korne. So, you and your guns back off,' Wesley threatened, drawing away towards the batwings.

Korne moved quickly after him, reaching out for a

grip on his shoulder. But Wesley expected the move and allowed himself to be pulled around. He lashed out at Korne's face, drove his balled fist hard into the man's mouth and nose. Blood spurted immediately and Korne reeled away.

Wanting a decisive finisher, Wesley made a move forward, but when Korne lifted his bloodied face and drew back his arm, common sense checked him.

'I'm unarmed, Korne,' he said, spitting out the words angrily. 'That's all you're getting from me, this night.'

But already, Bass had moved quickly to bar his way, and he had a gun in his fist. 'You stay one way or another,' the big half-breed warned.

Behind him, Wesley sensed the movement of Korne's lunging attack, and cursing, he swung around to meet him. 'If you don't *listen*, you have to *feel*, goddamn it,' he snarled, ducking as Korne's bony fist grazed his temple. He swung a short, hard right into Korne's middle, and the man jack-knifed. He grunted with satisfaction and straightened up as Korne again reeled away.

The man was hurt, but his reactions were undimmed. Hauling in the air that had been knocked from him, he came back, battering into Wesley's chest with his head lowered. Taking a hard thump, Wesley staggered away, until the back of his legs struck a table and he fell sideways to the floor.

With his bloodied mouth fixed in a gory snarl, Korne went after him. But Wesley twisted violently, and Korne's boot missed its target. Korne took thin air and momentarily lost his balance, toppling over Wesley's body as he too went down with a gasp and a dull thud.

Wesley clambered to his feet, took a blow straight in the face from Mose Parker who, waiting for the opportunity, had closed in.

Wesley felt the salt taste of blood in his mouth. His head was reeling as he raised his hands, backing away.

Korne got to his feet and pushed Parker away. 'Leave him to me,' he snarled, moving towards Wesley.

Wesley knew he could take Korne, but it wouldn't be over. If he downed him, Parker would take up the fight. Maybe Bass would get involved too, whether it was necessary or not. He threw a glance at the crowd that had formed a ragged ring around them, sensed that no one would be getting involved. They didn't know the grounds, and aggravating three armed strangers was risky. Sending a runner to the sheriff's office wouldn't be good for him, either. It would probably put an end to the fight, but if Rufus Tendecker arrested him for a breach of the peace, or some such civil disorder, the records from Yuma's State Prison would almost certainly make an appearance.

Wesley stood against the wall, his head clearing. A moment later, he flicked his head to one side as Korne's left arm pistoned at him.

Korne uttered a cry of pain when his fist cracked into the solid, planked wall. Grabbing the back of a chair, Wesley took a step forward. He swung it hard at Mose Parker who was trying to cut off his escape. Parker yelled when he got hit, cursing as he fell to his knees. Wesley whirled around, unleashed a power-house fist that caught the lunging Korne between the eyes, above his great, beaked nose.

Korne snorted with pain, reeled away half stunned and temporarily blinded by the flash of lights in his head. He lashed out blindly with his left, then his right, felt the solid contact with flesh and bone against his fist.

Shaking his head, blinking to bring clearness back, Wesley moved up close to Korne. He twisted to one side, bringing his knee up hard, low into Korne's belly. He didn't see the man hit the floor. He was ducking and continuing to turn as Bass bore down on him.

'I knew it,' Wesley rasped. 'You sons-of-bitches only swoop on carrion.' He edged around a table, in one quick movement, lifted the edge and rammed it hard and straight at the big half-breed. Bass stumbled backwards, grunted with pain and shouted something at Parker.

Wanting to get out into the street, Wesley tried to avoid Parker. As he swerved around a vicious low kick, Bass moved to bar his route to the batwings. Korne was getting groggily to his feet.

Hemmed in now, Wesley moved back. Then he turned and ran for the side door he'd seen on the opposite side of the bar to where he stood drinking. He wrenched it open.

Breathing heavily, he slammed the door closed behind him and blundered into semi-darkness. He was standing on a square landing that had a flight of steps leading up to the saloon's first floor. His immediate impulse was to rush into the alley, but he knew he'd be caught by Bass before he'd got to the main street and made fifty yards. *And now he'll probably use his goddamn gun,* he thought cynically, leaping for the wooden steps.

He stood panting on the upper landing, having raced as light-footed as he could up the dozen or so steps. Below him, the saloon's side-door flew open and he pressed himself flat against the wall. Not daring to move or enter the building's upper rooms, he saw the big shadowy figure of Bass stagger past in the gloom below. Moments later, the squat figure of Mose Parker showed. The man stopped for a moment and listened, then followed Bass towards the main street.

Wondering if Farley Korne would show, Wesley

14

took a few, deep, calming breaths. If Bass and Parker didn't hear or see anything quickly, would they turn back to the saloon for a closer look? *No, they'll scour the back alleys for a while. So, maybe I'll get in here and take a room,* he thought, wryly.He reached for the handle of the door beside him, gulping with surprise when the door opened unexpectedly.

Wesley drew back his fist, was preparing to drive it into Korne's tough face once again, when the girl appeared silently in the doorway. She was wearing a short, yellow dress and her shoulders were bare. That much, Wesley could see in the dim light. He cursed silently, staring at her fearful, pale face. But the shortest moment later, he came to and took a step forward and gripped her firmly around the waist. He clamped his other hand to her mouth, choking back the cry that he couldn't risk.

2

Wesley saw light coming from the half open door of one of the rooms. 'I guess that's where you come from,' he said, almost lifting the girl from the floor. He half-carried her to the room and kicked the door shut behind him, holding her firmly as he spoke.

'I'm sorry Miss,' he mumbled through his swollen lips. 'I'm in a spot of trouble. I'm not going to hurt you, so please don't scream or holler when I let you go. You're not going to, are you?'

The girl's eyes were gleaming dark with anger, but she shook her head.

Wesley released her, watching her warily as she moved away from him, smoothing down the front of her skimpy dress.

Through his half-closed, bloodshot eyes, he was aware of her striking appearance. She was small, but her eyes were big, brown and lustrous, and her very long hair was raven. He had never seen her before, but then, he had never seen any of the saloon girls, let alone touch or talk to them. He was always long gone by the time the nightly carousing started.

Wesley reeled as he moved towards her. In the perceptible shelter, he was suddenly near to collapse. The inside of his head was still thumping and he put out a hand to steady himself against the wall.

'Yeah, I'm sorry,' he repeated. 'I've met the town toughs. There were three of them, and I was worried they'd use their guns. All I had was an assortment of tables and chairs.'

The anger in the girl's dark eyes faded at Wesley's brief explanation, at the sight of his evident wounding. 'Sit on the bed before you collapse on to it,' she said. 'You can tell me the full story afterwards if you want. You're not wearing a gun, so unless you're the Black Mesa Strangler. . . .'

'No, I'm not him, Miss. I was just trying to get away.'

One of Wesley's eyes was almost completely closed behind a big purpling bruise. He only had a slitted, bleary view of her as she poured water from a pitcher into a hand basin, taking a bottle and a jar from a drawer in the wash-stand and bringing it over to him.

He tensed when the strong, antiseptic-smelling water bit into the wound around his mouth. Then he calmed a little, as with more gentle movements, the girl bathed the swelling around his eyes.

'And this shirt's got to come off,' she said. 'I don't often get to unbutton a feller who's name I don't know.'

'I'm Wesley Teal. And the last time this happened to me, it was my ma, and I was probably six or seven.'

'Yeah I bet. Lift your arms,' she replied.She pulled off his undershirt and, eyeing his bare chest, pursed her lips to suck in a little air.

Wesley gasped at the movement, protesting slightly as he squinted down at the dark bruises where Farley Korne had butted him.

The girl cleaned the bruising, and as she bent over him, he felt the warmth of her, the spicy scent of her body. In spite of his discomfort, he felt a sudden desire, oddly ashamed at wanting to reach out and draw her to him. *Jesus, if only old Poke could see me now,* he thought.

As though she had somehow sensed what was in Wesley's mind, the girl looked up. 'I guess you'll mend,' she said. 'I'll rub in some of this ointment.' Her cool, soft fingers worked over the bruises on his chest and those on his face, then she helped him back on with his shirt.

'Just out of interest, what is this stuff you've smeared me with?' he asked.

'Amy's magical elixir of face paint and lard. It's the horse liniment that stings though,' she added with a wry, lingering smile. 'You'd be surprised at what girls like me collect on our travels. Do you reckon it's working?'

'Yeah, I reckon. Thanks,' Wesley replied, returning the smile. 'Amy?' he asked.

'Ameline Chard. Pleased to meet you, Wesley. It's none of my business . . . well, it is a bit . . . but why would these men beat you up so?' she asked.

Wesley considered for a moment. 'They've been treading on my tail for a while. My time was up, I guess.'

'Fair enough,' Amy said and nodded agreeably. 'I've seen you around, haven't I . . . at the livery?'

'Yeah, possibly. Not any more though.'

'You're leaving? Because of those men?'

'In the circumstances, what would you do?' Wesley said, with a painful grimace.

'I know that if it takes three of them, they've got to be bluff and bluster. More hat than cattle, my pa would have said.'

'Huh. Ma's and pa's have this habit of telling kids stuff that turns out to be as worthless as barrels full of shucks.'

'Well, if it's as bad as that, won't they just chase you to the next town along the line? If they were going to kill you, wouldn't they have done it already?'

'Maybe. There were a few witnesses around,' Wesley agreed. 'And I am worth something to them

19

alive. For a while, anyways.'

'How long have they been after you?'

'Five years.'

Amy's eyes blinked with surprise. 'You've been running for five years?'

'Yeah. But I spent a lot of it circling the dirt yards of Yuma Penitentiary,' Wesley said, a thin, bitter smile twisting his damaged mouth. 'I guess they had someone inside who told them when I got released.'

'Oh, I see.' Amy looked at him hopefully, waiting for him to say more. But he didn't. 'Well, I have to go shortly,' she then added, her tone a little flatter. 'I'm paid to be in the saloon.'

'Yeah, of course you are. I'll get myself together, and leave the same way I came,' Wesley said awkwardly. 'I'd like to see you again, for proper thanking, you know.'

'No, I'm not sure that I do. But it's best you stay here, until I come back,' Amy responded firmly.

'How can I do that?'

'You lay down and close your eyes for a few hours, that's how. Not that you could manage much else. Besides those men will still be around. I won't be back until midnight at the earliest, and you can move out then, if you want.'

'You're being mighty accommodating,' Wesley said. 'I didn't figure on any of this.'

'I know you didn't.' Amy lifted a lace mantilla

from the back of a chair. 'The key's inside the door, so just lock it when I go out. It'll be around midnight, when I knock, so don't lie awake waiting for me.' She opened the door and peered out. 'And try taking those boots off,' she added, giving him a quick, reassuring smile. 'I can't do everything for you.'

Wesley watched Amy's slight figure as she walked to the head of the steps. After closing and locking the door behind him, he cursed and groaned at pulling off his boots, then stretched out on the bed.

3

Some discomfort and dull pain were still there, but Wesley was more relaxed. He looked up at the raftered ceiling, then around the room that, without Amy's presence, somehow now looked dismal and depressing. There was an attempt at decoration with rose bouquets on the faded wallpaper, and a similar pattern on skimpy curtains. The floor covering was floral too, with small red flowers strewn across a background that was once yellow. *Just as well I'm not ill,* Wesley thought. As tiredness began its subtle work, the strains of a piano drifted up from the saloon, and he conjured up an image of Amy dancing with cowpunchers and miners. *Most of them will be half-drunk, and got their arms around her,* his weary thoughts continued. *Hell of a goddamn job.*

It was a new and curiously exciting situation for Wesley. Thinking of the indignities that Amy would probably have to put up with, he moved restlessly on the bed. Girls hadn't played much of a part in his life. He had only been eighteen when he went to prison, and up until then, he'd never lived in a town as long as he had in Mariposa, let alone make a liaison.

All his life he had been on the move, his only home being a creaking old Pitt schooner. His pa would be up on the driving seat, and he'd be alongside riding a bay saddler. When they had taken over the sod-roofed shack at Calido Run, his ma had worked hard at making a permanent home. But her time had run out by then, and with each succeeding year, his pa had become more remote and withdrawn.

In a prelude to sleep, Wesley's mind began to wander and he was seeing overlapping images of his parents. Romanticism was being suffused with reality, when an insistent knocking on the door stirred him awake. The oil lamp was still burning on a low wick, and he realized he'd been in a deep sleep. He grunted involuntarily, as the movement of raising himself brought deep stabs of pain across his chest. Resorting to vital curses, he eased himself from the bed and stepped tentatively towards the door.

'Who is it?' he asked with tired, careless thought.

'Me. It's me, Amy. Let me in.'

'Do you feel any better?' Amy's dark eyes looked up inquiringly as Wesley locked the door behind her.

'You look as though you've just woken up.'

'Ha! Yeah, reckon I might have dozed off for a few minutes,' he answered, tempering the fact. 'What time is it?'

'About half an hour after midnight.'

Wesley saw the tiredness of her then. It showed in her eyes, her movement as she walked slowly to the dressing table. 'You look like how I was feeling earlier,' he said. 'Sorry, I don't mean that the way it sounds,' he added quickly and embarrassed. 'I mean, what do you do all this time? Sorry, I didn't mean that either.'

'It's my job, Wesley. I make some dollars from it.'

'Yeah, of course. It's just from the way you talk . . . nice like.'

'That's a privilege of being sent east for an education. Even though it was cut short. My pa wanted to keep me away while he drank himself into oblivion. But there's nothing particularly strange about me working here. My ma did.'

'What happened to them?'

'Ma ran for the hills, eventually. Pa was a stock agent, but when he lost his business, he took a job as swamper in this very saloon. At least he was close to what he really loved.' Amy smiled wistfully. 'He died about a year ago. So as I said, I'm a natural, and that's about all there is to know about me.'

In spite of his newly awakened feelings, Wesley

couldn't break open the five year crust of cautious reserve. But Amy had helped him. She had a soft body, smelled good and he wanted more.

'I guess I'd better be moving on,' he heard himself saying. Immediately, he saw the disappointment, thinking perhaps Amy wanted some reciprocal confidence.

'Everyone's talking about you,' she said. 'You hurt two of those men pretty badly. They were in the saloon when I left. The other one had to have the doc look at him. So, I suppose if you want to ride that thing they call the owl-hoot, then now's your chance.'

'I only came to Mariposa for a stopover when I came out of prison, Amy. I didn't think you wanted an explanation,' he said defensively. 'And most folk would have wanted to know about Yuma. You didn't.'

'What's to ask about?' Amy replied. 'A killer's the worst thing you could be, but you wouldn't be in this room now, if I really thought you were.'

'Yeah, well I'm not. I did kill a man, but I'm not a killer. I guess you're looking at the difference.'

Amy gave a short, brittle laugh. 'I know what I'm looking at, Wesley. It's a saloon girl's lot,' she said sadly. She looked completely bewildered, and there were tears glistening in her big eyes. 'So, go if you're going,' she said, turning her head away. 'I'm tired, it's late and it's *my* bed.'

Wesley stared down at the girl's flushed face. He reached out and gripped her arms, drawing her closer. He felt her stiffen, and with a quick movement he released her, slipping his own arms around her body.

'But I want to see you again, Amy,' he started huskily. 'I'm coming back, believe me. If I'm known for anything since coming to Mariposa, it's keeping my word.' He raised her face to look up at him and immediately kissed her. He felt the tautness leave her body, yielding against his own. The soft warmth of her lips was enthralling, but then she hardened again, and her hands pressed against his chest.

'Please, just go,' she said, moving away from him, taking rapid breaths. 'Call it, *hasta la vista.*'

'I'm in love with you, Amy,' he exclaimed, without warning.

'Oh Wesley. It's not love. You're infatuated, maybe grateful as well. It's a powerful blend, but it's not love. Not in an hour, believe me.'

'You don't want to see me again? Is that it?' he asked, with a shade of anxiety.

'No, Wesley, hasta la vista doesn't mean that. I think you're a good man, and I believe everything you've told me. But you've got to get yourself sorted before making talk like that.'

'I can't help it, Amy. It's more than talk. It's like a thunderbolt.' The words came tumbling out, surprising

26

Wesley himself.

'It's a lovely compliment, and I'm touched. I really am, Wesley. But with things the way they are, nothing can come of it.'

On impulse, Wesley made a grab for her. She backed off, but he caught her, held her tightly while his lips eagerly sought hers again. She resisted, but it was brief, and her arms went almost involuntarily around his neck.

When their embrace quietened, Wesley held her in his arms, her head gentle against his chest. 'Something can come of it, if you want. I know how *I* feel,' he said, more sensitively.

'You're real fine, Wesley, but you've got to lift yourself from whatever mess you're in. If you still feel the same way after, come calling. I'd like to see you again, I really would. I won't be going anywhere,' Amy said, trying to calm the proddy atmosphere.

'I'm going to Calido Run,' he said resolutely. 'There's something that's been at the back of my mind for five years, and now I've got a reason to go back and deal with it. I can't explain, but I reckon if I can avoid trouble, there'll be a big difference in my prospects. I'd like a chance to share them with you, Amy.'

'And what happens if you *don't* avoid trouble?'

'That'll be for them that cause it to worry about. Now I know what I want, I aim to make the right and

27

proper play.'

For a moment, Amy looked as though she was about to ask a question, but changed her mind. 'You'd better go before those men leave the saloon all liquored up,' she said, offering a weak smile.

The top of the steps were now in complete darkness, and she listened for a moment before raising her face. 'Be real careful, Wesley Teal,' she whispered. 'I want to know more about those prospects.'

4

Moving vigilantly, Wesley made his way to the end of the lane. He crossed the main street, then along a narrow alleyway until he reached a clap-boarded building, rising high and dark in the moonlight. He went through the back gate of the livery, crossing the yard where a few old wrecked carts and wagons lay heaped like skeletons.

The rear entrance to the livery had no doors, simply led past a line of stalls to the front of the building. Wesley's quarters were on the upper floor with the lofts, and reached by a ladder inside the gateway. He could see a dim light from the harness room, where Poke Lemmer was dozing. He climbed the ladder, flicked a match at the top, and went into his cramped quarters. It was a coffin of a room, occupied almost entirely by a bunk. There was a chest of drawers with a shaving mirror and a stool at one end, and a door at the other. Months earlier, Lemmer had told Wesley he'd stopped climbing up to the room himself, because when he came through the door and saw his reflection in the mirror he almost fell straight back down the ladder. He hadn't been too keen on bats, either, and rats and roaches were skilled climbers.

Wesley lit a small oil lamp on the chest, dragged open its bottom drawer and took out an oiled paper parcel. He unwrapped a filled gunbelt that was coiled around a Colt's .44 revolver and holster.

It had taken most of his first month's wages at the livery. He'd practised regularly most mornings, taking a long ride out of town in the early hours. He had become accustomed to the weight and balance of the gun, achieving a fair degree of accuracy, and he'd oiled and worked out the stiff newness of the holster. He didn't have the speed of a professional gunhand, but had learned that accuracy was more important. 'Surprise is good when your luck's down,' he'd once heard a murderous inmate advise.

He buckled the gunbelt around his waist, and looked around the room. There was little else for him to take, except a few spare clothes which he wrapped in his slicker roll. He also owned a horse and a saddle, that, together with the Colt, were just about all he'd gained from three months hard work at the livery. But they were crucial, the reason for his taking on the job before riding to Calido Run. Poke Lemmer wouldn't be happy about his abrupt departure, but the timing wasn't of Wesley's doing, and perhaps not so much when weighed against a five year wait. He blew out the lamp and quit the room that had been his home. He went down the ladder and padded his way across the dark earth floor to one of two side rooms.

Wrapped in a heavy blanket coat, Lemmer was deep in rough-and-ready slumber. His feet were up on the crude desk, and short, sharp snores disturbed the quietness.

'Some things don't change,' Wesley muttered as he shook the old man's shoulder. 'Sorry to wake you, Poke, but I'm pulling out,' he said.

Lemmer grunted, catching his breath, and opening one bleary eye. 'Is that you, Wesley?' he retorted, snorting himself awake. 'Goddamn it, I wait months for somethin', then you come up with this.' He swung his feet to the floor, kneaded his eyeballs with his knuckles. 'What the hell are you up to, boy? An' what's the goddamn time?'

'It's after midnight, Poke. I'm sorry about leaving in such a hurry, but something's come up, and I've got to go.'

'Huh. Must be the hounds of hell.'

'Yeah, something like that, Poke, but I'll be back. That's a promise,' he added, his thoughts more for

31

Ameline Chard than Poke Lemmer.

'What sort o' business you got? No, don't tell me, you're workin' on somethin',' Lemmer suggested, wryly.

'Yeah, that's right, Poke. Now I've got to saddle up.'

'You can't just up an' leave. It ain't right,' Lemmer protested peevishly, ever frustrated in his attempt to learn something of the remote young hostler.

'An' what's that goddamn hogleg you're wearin'?' he grunted, seeing the Colt that Wes was now carrying. 'Just where do you think you're goin'?'

'Some place, Poke. Some place. You coming to help me?' Wesley walked briskly past the stables to the saddle store, went in and lit the hanging lantern. He hauled out the time-worn gear he'd bought from Lemmer, carried it across to the stalls and saddled and bridled his mare.

Looking glum, Lemmer walked with Wesley to the entrance. 'So you really are goin'?' he said, shoving out a horny hand. 'You only been here a short while an' I still don't know more'n spit about you. You've got chops tighter'n a viper's ass, that's for sure.'

Wesley smiled awkwardly at Lemmer's sincerity. 'Thanks Poke,' he said, 'I reckon that's your way of trying to say you'll miss me. But I've got good reason. You'll get your big windy, when I come back.'

'OK.' Lemmer's expression became a shy, leathery

grin. 'I'll be holdin' you to it. Besides, who's to do all the heavy liftin'?'

'You'll find some other bone-head. And get yourself a dog,' Wesley said, releasing his grip on Lemmer's hand. He was considering saying why he had good reason to return, but instead, he turned to his horse. He gripped the saddle horn and immediately went very still, cursed silently as he saw a massive figure loom in the entrance.

'Stand away, Teal, an' lift your hands.' Bass's words were brittle as he stepped forward, his sixgun gleaming in the spread of lamp light. 'You too, *viejo*,' he said, flicking his gun to cover Lemmer.

It was the merest shift of the half-breed's attention, but it was a slim chance to Wesley, maybe the only one, and instinct told him to take advantage. Stepping clear of the horse, and with his arms still raised, he took one fast step forward and hurled himself downwards. His outstretched hands grasped at Bass's legs, who, uttering a venomous curse, went over backwards.

Bass's gun exploded towards the roof and Wesley's horse snorted in fear. It reared and pawed the air, its hoofs thudding down close to Wesley's sprawled body.

The half-breed, flat on his back, kicked out, and Wesley released his legs and rolled across the dark, reeking ground. With an agility remarkable for a big man, Bass sprung back to standing. His gun roared again, the sound reverberating madly in the cavernous space.

But Wesley was already clear, and now making a grab for Lemmer. He pulled and twisted the old man, and together they went crashing through the door of the saddle room. 'Get down and stay there,' Wesley yelled. 'Go back to sleep, I'll take care of it.'

Wesley turned out the oil lamp, and drawing his Colt, moved the door to half closed, with the toe of his boot. Standing silent, he peered into the darkness, straining his ears, breathing fast and shallow. His mare had galloped back to the yard, swelling the wild disturbance from the stalls, the thudding of restless hoofs, and terrified whinnying.

Wesley steadied his gun against the doorframe and waited. Bass was out of the light, but Wesley saw the quick, shadowy movement as the man crossed the livery entrance. He squeezed the trigger, but the preceding silence had given too much of his intention away and the half-breed had sensed it.

Bass turned, dropped to one knee as Wesley's bullet thumped into the side wall. Then he was gone, out into the darkness and safety of the street.

Wesley ran for the door. For a moment, he heard the man's boots on a boardwalk, then silence. He thought he saw a movement on the opposite side of the street and raised his Colt, but a store awning

34

cloaked everything in deep shadow. He held himself very still against the livery wall, his eyes straining, probing the spot where Bass had disappeared.

There was a shout from the opposite direction and he swivelled around towards the lights from Sappers Hole. There were a few silhouetted figures between the batwings and the hitchrail, late drinkers disturbed and excited by the shooting. Then he saw the tall figure walking purposefully down the boardwalk and he ground his jaw. The man was Rufus Tendecker, the sheriff.

Wesley switched his gaze backwards and forwards from where he'd seen Bass, to the advancing sheriff. He cursed. Three months out of Yuma and he was about to tangle with the law again. It would mean being dumped back into that hell-hole again, whatever the rights and wrongs of this night's business. He was on parole and he'd broken it. A charge of disturbing the peace would be enough to rob him of two years while he finished his original sentence.

He caught sight of the shadowy figure of Bass, who was now almost opposite him. He edged back from the doorway, his main thought now to get away and clear of the town. 'Shame there weren't any elders or cubs here. You could probably have dealt with them,' he rasped scornfully as Bass's gun roared. With his eyes locked in to the gun flash, he fired twice. A moment later, Bass lurched from the boardwalk, raised a defiant hand, before sprawling headlong down to the street.

'You in the livery – drop the goddamn gun,' Tendecker shouted angrily.

Wesley ignored the sheriff's command and ducked back inside. He heard more raised voices, cursed loudly as two gunshots blasted into the walls of the livery.

'Korne and Parker,' Wesley seethed as he ran to the end of the livery. His horse was out in the yard, and it shied away nervously. He cornered it, muttered comforting sounds before grabbing at the bridle. He led the horse through the yard, out through the small gate which he'd left open. He leapt into the saddle and outside of the gate, kicked his heels, hard. The mare went into a gallop along the narrow lane, swung off at the town's limits and headed due north.

Wesley wondered whether he'd killed Jack Bass. If he had, he was standing deep in the molasses barrel. He'd be running from the law with Korne and Parker knowing where he was headed. Well perhaps not, he thought. It wouldn't be in their interests to have him tossed into jail or to be hanged, even. 'Yeah, thanks boys,' he muttered. 'Him who fights and runs away, eh?'

So now he was heading for the place that he'd been dreaming of for so long. Calido Run was a place of harsh memories and sadness, but now it held real hope for the future.

5

Wesley's jaw clamped hard when he recalled Calido Run. It had been the place of hope, of real achievement for his father, Austen. It was where the Teal family had put down roots, living in a house on the outskirts of the town, even though it was nothing more than a shanty with a brush shelter out back. But to the unimaginable relief of Martha Teal, it had been a fixed home after all those years of living in trail wagons.

Wesley's prevailing memory of his father was of a man obsessed by the lure of gold, always on the move towards that glistening horizon. He'd slaved over worthless, petered-out holes until he was forced to take a job, any job, when he couldn't get someone to grubstake him. Wesley had thought many times that it must have been worn out desperation that made his mother finally refuse to move on.

So, it was decided. Austen would temporise with Calido Run. They would settle in the shack that he had purchased for the *next-to-nothing* he had scraped together. In the gulch, there were men who eked out a living from placer gold. It wasn't much of an existence, but there was always the chance of raking up something bigger. Where there were grains there could be nuggets. And it wasn't like having to dig in flinty ground, blasting rocks apart. And if all that failed, the territory supported many livestock ranches, and Austen Teal did have a way with horses – a quality he had passed on to his son.

So Martha Teal went along with that. She would have gone along with anything that gave her a home that wasn't situated above the screech and lurch of a wheel axle.

Young Wesley had taken odd jobs around the town, while, true to form, Austen moved out to work along the gulch. He could be gone for a few days or a few weeks, but he would always return with a meagre poke. On one occasion, he had bought a feather bonnet for Martha. It was a pretty gift, but no more than a pitiful offering to temper another barren trip. It was down to Wesley's few, hard-earned dollars to supply the necessities.

To begin with, Wesley's mother had shared her husband's fervor, but the restless years of living on the edge of depredation had taken its toll. Three months after the Teals had settled in Calido Run, she died in her sleep. 'She's just too worn out to wake up,' Wesley overheard a neighbour mutter.

The crowning irony was that Austen Teal was about to realize his life's dream. He had struck gold, a rich deposit. He came back with the news two days after Wesley had buried Martha.

The meeting with his father came back in a vivid rush, as Wesley rode through the night. Usually, Austen was cagey, even secretive, but the strike had been too much for him. After a two-week-long raging thirst, he had stumbled into the saloon. His mistake had been paying for his drink with a small nugget, then accepting what the barkeep chose to give him in change. But then, he had pushed the money back and called for drinks for everyone. 'Beers on me,' he'd said. 'Beers on me, boys.'

The three men now on Wesley's trail, along with a man named Ike Wittman, had caught wind of the excitement, and made it to the saloon in quick time. One of the younger drinkers had run out to the Teal's shack. 'There's goin' to be trouble, boy, you best get there,' he had warned Wesley.

Wittman and Austen were arguing when Wesley arrived. Wittman was saying that he had grubstaked Austen, and was asking questions. But Austen said that the few bucks Wittman had loaned him was because he was down on his luck, and not a grubstake.

Just how the fight started remained a flawed blur in Wesley's mind. He had tried to get his pa away, told him to come home, but Ike Wittman had barred their way. Austen had panicked then. He drew his old Army revolver and without even raising the long barrel, he'd fired. It was a single shot, and smashed into Wittman's kneecap. The man gasped, drew his own Colt and shot Austen in the chest before collapsing to the floor with a harsh cry of agony.

Wesley lost his temper then. He grabbed up Austen's gun and shot Wittman at point blank range as he lay writhing and cursing.

Effectively preventing the advance of Wittman's three cohorts, the saloon crowd surged close. They created space for Wesley to drag his father out on to the planked walkway and helped to prop the old man against the low street steps. Wesley asked them to go get someone, a doctor, anyone, then watched forlornly as to a man, they pushed their way back through the saloon doors.

With his emotions numbed, Wesley put a supporting arm around his pa who was whispering hoarsely. There were few words, and 'Slingshot Creek' made little sense, but then Wesley realized it was most likely the location of the strike.

It was less than a minute later, when the tall, bearded figure of the sheriff came running. Grover Garve stepped from the street to the walkway.

41

Coming close, but not attempting to interfere, he leaned in to hear the last repeated words gasped out by Austen Teal before he died.

'What was that? He was tryin' to say somethin'.' Garve's voice was thick with anticipation as he bent down beside Wesley. 'He was tellin' you where there's gold,' he continued, gripping Wesley's shoulder. 'I ain't heard of any place called "Tortola Rocks", though. Where's he talkin' about, son?'

Wesley ground his jaw. 'I just shot one man, Sheriff, and I'll probably get to hang for it. But that's a thing they can only do once, so if you lay a hand on me again, or call me *son*. . . .' he replied, letting the words trail off, bitter and ominous.

From then on, Wesley didn't say any more. He kept his mouth shut. He couldn't, wasn't, going to trust Grover Garve, and had been summarily jailed for the killing of Ike Wittman. That was the start of another memory seared into Wesley's mind. Garve alone with him in the cell, arguing followed by plead-ing for a lead on the whereabouts of Tortola Rocks. Then finally the beatings when the man's patience gave out. In Yuma, after he was sentenced, Wesley bore a long harboured revenge against the brutal lawman. But he learned about time, and eventually his thoughts turned to the fortune waiting for him somewhere along Calido Gulch. On reflection, he had few doubts about his pa's find. Austen Teal had spent too many years of dedicated searching to be fooled by an odd grain, even a nugget or two. Wesley knew the gold was there, near a secret place the old man had called Tortola Rocks. It would be some sort of payback for five years of hard labour and keeping quiet. Now all he had to do was find it. *Maybe if I had the help of Amy Chard,* he mused.

Wesley spent the night under the stars, but he'd been riding a full hour before the first colours spread from the east, cracking open the darkness.

At midday, he rested for an hour. The sun was high and brassy, and he took shade under a creekside willow. An hour later he pushed on, hitting the rise above Calido Run in late afternoon.

He was overlooking the town from the western end. Spread out before him, he could see roofs of all shapes and sizes, but it was bigger, more sprawling than he recalled. More solid buildings stood where once there had been false-fronted constructions with canvas roofs and walls. The older town looked familiar, but that was immediately below. At the eastern end, Wesley traced the main street, saw it had pushed through what had been nothing more than a trail bounded by brush and scrub oak. Then his gaze moved beyond the town to the north. That was Calido Gulch territory, where craggy hills and mountains formed walls rising in tiers above the creek.

That wouldn't have changed, and somewhere along the many miles of winding, fast, running water, was a place that Austen Teal had called Tortola Rocks.

As Wesley carefully rode his mare down the hillside, he wondered if the name of Teal would still be remembered. The killings had been a big thing at the time, but with all the outcasts and rake-hell folk that such a frontier town attracted, it wasn't such a remarkable event that it wouldn't be worsted by the next outbreak of violence. But gold was a different matter. It wasn't called 'the devil's fish hook' for nothing. All the same, Wesley was hopeful that his pa's claim had been received as nothing more than wishful thinking, and gold hunters would have long given up the search. That meant the only trouble would be from the three men still on his trail. Them, and Grover Garve.

Wesley scowled, wondering if Garve was still the sheriff of Calido Run. From the look of it, a bullying, scheming, crooked lawman wouldn't have been fundamental to the town's civic improvements. Well he'd soon know. And he didn't want to hang around. A few essential provisions and he'd be starting his move along the gulch.

6

At the foot of the slope, Wesley swung into the main
street. Now, it had a sign that stated it was 'Main
Street', and he gave a wry smile. The part of the town
he'd known appeared mostly unchanged, more
familiar than the overall spread. Doves Mercantile
looked the same as it always did. The shrewd propri-
etor had clearly built with an eye to the future.
Reckoning on the growth of the town, the big, white-
fronted building with its large, plate-glass windows
remained an affecting structure.

There was some activity at that time of day with the
lessening of the heat bringing out a few shoppers,
pedestrians on the boardwalk, buggies in the yellow-
dusted street moving slowly along Main, one or two
riders. There would be more activity after dusk, when
cowpunchers came in for the evening.

No one paid much attention to the tall, young

Wesley as he dismounted at the hitch rail outside the mercantile. With his head lowered, he went into the comparative cool dimness of the store.

To Wesley's eyes, Armstrong Dove had hardly changed a day. The bald-headed storekeeper with a white apron was talking to a middle-aged woman across the counter on which were stacked bolts of material. A man who was obviously the woman's husband was beside the cracker barrel, helping himself, bored with waiting. Wesley recognized the man, almost remembered his name. The man stopped champing and looked at Wesley, and Wesley nodded. A moment later he turned back to the counter where Dove was measuring out the brightly checkered material the woman had chosen.

The man at the cracker barrel continued to stare at Wesley, until the spark of recognition appeared in his blue, watery eyes. And with it came a glint of expectation.

The woman completed her purchases and moved to the door, stood there waiting impassively. The man took another cracker from the barrel and came across, his eyes still fixed on Wesley.

'Hello, Mr Dove,' Wesley said, placing a short list of basic foodstuffs on to the counter. 'Do you remember me?'

The storekeeper stared at Wesley for a long moment, then his bemused expression changed.

46

'Well I'll be. Wesley Teal. It's been a while.' He gripped Wesley's offered hand, shook it genuinely.

'Yep, I thought so,' the man at the doorway said to his wife. 'Ol' Austen Teal's boy. You remember him, Bea? He was the one who . . ..' But his words trailed away as the couple left the store.

'Well it's good to see you, Wesley,' the storekeeper reacted warmly. 'You just got out?' he went on quickly, eyeing Wesley's pale face. 'You should never have been in, from what I heard. I hope it didn't sour you too much. If I've learned anything in life, it's put bad stuff behind you.'

'Yeah, good sentiment, Mr Dove. Might work for tiffs and flour talleys, but I did five years in the Yuma pen,' Wesley replied.

'Hmm, so what's brought you back?' Dove asked.

Wesley frowned, thought for a second. 'Well, it's like what you heard, Mr Dove. I shouldn't ever have been in there,' he said. 'And I reckon you're the sort of man who doesn't usually ask a question unless he already knows the answer.'

Dove nodded sternly at Wesley's reckoning. 'The story of your pa's gold was a real Pandora's box, Wesley, and caused a lot of trouble one way and another. I hope you ain't here to stir things up.'

'No, I'm not, Mr Dove, believe me. But if there's something that involves my pa, how can it be anyone's business but mine?'

47

'True, but you haven't exactly been around to make it yours,' Dove started off. 'Besides, you know something of these misguided fortune hunters. They'll keep any story alive if it involves gold, even more so if it becomes a myth. For five years, there's been men prowling the gulch, working any likely-looking gravel bed and sandbank. Nothing's been left to chance, and nothing that hasn't been dug up or blown up. Huh, with fights and killings, there's more wayside graves than gold seams.'

'Yeah, I can imagine,' Wesley affirmed quietly and reminiscent. 'It takes the kind of stupidity you'd credit their mules with.'

'Well it's so, Wesley. Perhaps there's not so much fight left in them, but they're still searching, and it wouldn't take much to start trouble. Grover Garve's one of them. He's never given up.'

'Grover Garve,' Wesley repeated the name, inner rage and resentment instantly surging through him. *So he's here after all,* he thought, recalling the promises and the propositions and the beatings once meted out by the town's sheriff. 'I remember him. A fine upholder of the law.'

'He was an upholder of something. But with the law's stretching it,' Dove said knowingly. 'And the gold cost him his job and near most of his wits.'

'But he's still around?'

'Sure. But like I say, he's struck by the fever – as

48

crazy as the worst of them. He got so he couldn't think of anything but that gold. For some reason he reckoned he had a better idea of where your pa made his find, and neglected his job because of it. Things got so bad that the town councillors got together and hoisted him out of office. Now we've got Vern Howell . . . used to be top hand out on the Broomtail.'

'And Grover Garve's looking for my pa's find, you say?' Wesley was thinking back to the time outside of Sappers Hole, when Garve heard his pa mention Tortola Rocks. 'So how's he making out if he's no job, presumably no grubstake?'

'He's got a partner. You remember Beaver John?'

Wesley nodded. 'I remember his smell.'

Beaver John had always been an infrequent visitor in town. He wore fringed buckskins, was very hairy and smelled like a bitch's litter; a memorable character for an impressionable youngster. 'Sometimes a bit o' trapping in between mining, an' sometimes a bit o' mining in between trapping,' he'd once said when Wesley asked him what he did and where he went.

'Beaver John and Grover Garve are partners?' Wesley queried. 'Are you sure, Mr Dove? That's a nasty picture to go to sleep on.'

Dove smiled in agreement. 'They do a bit of panning . . . placer stuff, but they're sniffing down that lode.'

Wesley drew a long breath. He was sure the speculation of his pa's strike was all but forgotten. But it was clear that because of Grover Garve's relentless search, it remained a story with legs at Calido Run.

'It sounds to me like you've got a score to settle,' Dove commented, as though divining Wesley's mind. 'You certainly ain't here to buy candy. Do you think your pa really did find something along the gulch? Is that it, Wesley?'

'No, nothing like it. I came for the candy,' Wesley said, returning a thin smile. 'Even so, I'd take kindly to that staying between us, Mr Dove.'

'The secret of your sweet tooth's safe with me, Wesley, but I'm afraid being in town's not. That feller who was in here when you arrived? He recognized you, and he's got a big maw on him. Unfortunately, so's his good wife,' Dove added as he looked past Wesley towards the big front window.

Wesley turned slowly, saw the man and his wife talking to an elderly couple on the pavement. Their conversation was animated, with surreptitious sideways glances into the store.

Suddenly, Wesley wanted to be clear of the town, its impulsive and meddlesome citizens. It would spread rapidly that Austen Teal's son was back, and he felt trapped. 'Goddamnit, this is just what I didn't want, Mr Dove,' he rasped. 'I had no idea this would likely happen. What's the matter with these people?

Haven't they got their own business to mind?'

'They have, but they want it laced. And they don't forget. Especially where gold's concerned.'

'Well, I'm riding out, Mr Dove,' Wesley said, taking another look at the folk on the pavement. 'I'll pick that coffee and stuff up from your yard, if that's OK?'

An approving glint came into Dove's eyes. 'Yeah, of course it's OK,' he returned with a wheezy chuckle. 'And don't worry. Those town jays'll get no chatter from me.'

'Thank you, Mr Dove.' Wesley pushed his hand into his pocket. 'I'll settle up now, if you don't mind.'

'Well I do. You can toss me some yellow grain when you next pass through.'

'I told you, *this* is what I came for,' Wesley said, pulling a stick of horehound candy from a jar.

7

Amy Chard spent a wakeful and restless night in her room. She heard the uproar in the street, the shots fired and the bellowing of Rufus Tendecker. It was with weary relief that she learned Wesley had got away. But feeling strangely deserted in the darkness of her room, she continued to worry, imagining all sorts of disasters about to befall him.

Later in the morning, she learned about the gun-fight in more detail. Wesley had shot the big half-breed known as Jack Bass, in the flesh of a side rib, and was the reason for the three men not to have gone straight into the chase, lawful or otherwise. Amy saw them talking and taking a drink in Sappers Hole. Bass had spent the night in the recovery room of the town doctor, and the other two had been forced to wait. It meant that Wesley had a good start, despite the fact that those in pursuit knew his desti-nation.

Amy felt drained, and the thought of nerve-racking days and nights ahead was making her deeply miserable. This man who had arrived so dramatically into her life, had inexplicably *become* her life. She believed Wesley Teal would come back for her, wanted it more than anything else in the world. But she couldn't wait for his return, and she made a decision. 'Sometimes you have to chase down what you want', her ma would have said. There was nothing to prevent her from going to Calido Run, and she guessed that Wesley would understand it.

One of the saloon girls, Felice Layber, had gone there more than a year ago when there were rumours of a strike in the gulch. Like many starry-eyed prospectors, Felice had figured that creek gold would ooze between your toes, that you'd exchange your pocketbook for a pail to carry it around town. It hadn't turned out that way, of course. The strike had produced nothing more than sand and bedrock and disillusioned panhandlers, but Felice had stayed on.

Amy didn't think there was any reason for her to stay in Mariposa, but now there was one for leaving. She could write and say there was an urgent and unexpected cause – which was arguably true. In terms of pay, her hasty departure would be mainly her loss, no one else's.

There was no direct route. Calido Run was a town on a spur trail, and required a change of coach on the journey from Mariposa. Excited, Amy packed a simple valise, and left with just enough time to catch the noon coach. She reached Viento Wells late that night, and stayed there until starting out on the second stage of her journey the following morning.

Arriving in Calido Run just before full dark, Amy felt a pang of unease when she stepped down from the coach into the glare of the oil lamps on the platform of the stage depot. The line agent looked up from the mails and parcels, and, not showing any curiosity, directed her to the Picture Paint Saloon.

She went through a set of double-doors into the hotel side of the building, booked a single room and asked after Felice Layber. The lobby clerk informed her that Miss Layber was indeed still booked in, and she thanked him, taking her key. As an afterthought she turned back. 'Is there a Mr Wesley Teal staying here?' she asked.

'Wes Teal? You know him?' the clerk, who had been watching her admiringly, replied.

'I asked if he was staying here,' Amy said, a little miffed at the man's interest.

'Sorry, I meant he's in town . . . not at the hotel though. Is this where you were to meet him?'

'Maybe,' Amy said. 'You obviously know him.' It was about all she could think of to allay the man's curiosity.

'I used to,' the clerk replied. 'But there's a lot o'

sand blown through here in five years. It's just that all of a sudden, most of the town's talkin' an' askin' about him.'

'Why's that?' Amy asked.

'Huh, if you don't know, ma'am, perhaps it ain't for me to say.' The clerk's awkwardness wasn't eased by his ogling smile.

Amy wanted to question him further, to find out what he was talking about, but she just returned his stare. She had taken an instant dislike to the man. Using experience gained from customers of Sappers Hole, she knew it would save her time.

'So, do you know where I can find him?' she asked as an alternative.

'No, just that he was in town. He was seen goin' into the mercantile, but he didn't talk to anyone except Armstrong Dove. He rode off soon after, an' that was about two hours ago, I guess. Maybe he's come back from where he was goin' an' takin' a drink.'

Amy let her eyes wander. She wondered if the person who had decorated the lobby had also been responsible for her room in Mariposa, and she smiled wryly.

'Why not take a look? It ain't that far to go.' The clerk nodded to a door almost opposite his cubby-hole reception. 'That takes you right in. Your friend Felice is probably in there too.'

'Thank you. I've only this valise with me. I'll leave it here, if I may.'

'You may, Miss Chard. And be careful. There's fellers in there who don't know a lady when they see one.'

Amy pushed against the heavy door and immediately a barrage of assorted sounds rolled towards her. She was accustomed to this sort of noisy conviviality, but now she felt nervous and unsure of herself. She peered through the haze of tobacco smoke and movement, looking to where the sound of a piano player came from. Avoiding eye contact, she moved towards the discordant jangling, trying not to notice the men and girls seated at the tables. Some of those standing were doing a shuffling, clumsy dance, more or less to the rhythm of the music.

The plumpish, blonde Felice Layber was in the arms of a lanky, solemn-faced man who looked like he could have been a rancher or a ranch foreman. He wasn't any sort of proficient dancer, stumbling forward, muttering sweet-nothings in her ear.

Amy waited until the music stopped, then she hurriedly edged through the separating couples. She called Felice's name and the girl turned quickly. 'Amy,' she said in instant recognition, closing in for a warm, spontaneous hug. 'Fancy you being here. Have you come for work?'

Amy shook her head and smiled. 'No, but you

never know. There's something I'd like to talk to you about, Felice. If you've got the time,' she added.

Felice nodded eagerly. 'This is Amy Chard from Mariposa,' she said soberly, looking to her dance partner. 'She's an old friend, and she's come to see me. Go get a drink, and I'll see you shortly.' Felice watched as the man mooched off obediently, then she took Amy's arm and led the way to an empty table.

As Amy sat down, she noticed that the hotel clerk was now standing in the doorway that led to and from the lobby. But when he caught her cold glare, he entered the saloon and walked up to the far end of the bar.

'You're not in any trouble, are you, Amy?' Felice, hurriedly wanted to know.

'No, I'm not in trouble, Felice. I'm here looking for a man.'

'Hah, take mine,' Felice replied with a chuckle. 'What are friends for?'

'This one's called Wesley Teal.'

'Wesley Teal,' Felice repeated. 'Well ain't that a name to side with.'

'What? What is this, Felice?' Amy demanded. 'First it's that creepy clerk, and now you're doing the same. What's so odd about Wesley Teal?'

Felice blinked then laughed. 'Nothing, Amy. But to come out with it so . . . so unabashed.'

With a look of exasperation now spreading across Amy's face, Felice continued, but more carefully. 'You really don't know, do you?' she said. 'You always were a bit different from the us other girls, Amy. You'd never play up to a feller, rich or poor.'

'What on earth are you talking about, Felice?'

'Money. I'm talking about Wesley Teal's money, or rather his gold. And if it's not his now, it soon will be. You don't know about it?'

'Of course not. I only know Wesley Teal, He said nothing about any gold, and I still don't know what you're talking about. He told me there was some business he had to attend to in Calido Run, that's about it.'

'They call it Teal's gold,' Felice said with an understanding smile. 'I guess if you'd lived here for a while you'd know what I'm talking about. The legend, if it is one, never stays silent for long.'

'My interest is with Wesley, and right now that's where it starts and finishes. As you seem to know so much else, Felice, perhaps you know where I can find him?'

'Well if he's here for his pa's gold, you'll not likely find him in town. He'll have moved out along the gulch.'

'His pa's gold?'

'Austen Teal. Years ago, it was him who made the discovery. Well, big old rumour says he did. He was killed after an argument about whether he'd been

58

grubstaked or not. The yarns, stories, call them what you like, fly thicker than mozzies. But from what I've heard, it seems there's some gunslicks trying to get their hands on the old man's find. Now you know about as much as I do, Amy.'

'Thank you. But how did *you* get to know it?'

'Oh Amy, how do you think? I'm a saloon girl.'

Amy nodded, smiled acceptingly as Felice continued.

'Apparently, one of them shot his father and Wesley . . . *your* Wesley, killed him for it. That's what he went to Yuma for. Grover Garve, who was the sheriff at the time, overheard something, and he's never stopped hunting the fortune he says is out there. At such times he has to, and to anyone who'll listen, he rants on about little else.' Amy tapped her temple with her finger. 'It's called oro loco. They call *him* the hombre loco.'

For a few moments, Amy sat in silence to gather her thoughts. She had an explanation for a state of affairs which, up until a few minutes ago, she hadn't known existed.

'You can't really do much more than wait, Amy,' Felice said. 'You can work here. It only takes a word from me, and the pay's good.'

'It's not what I came for.'

'You are the dark horse, aren't you? Have you any

59

idea what it's like out there in gulch country, Amy? You'd be at the mercy of all them gold grubbers. Anything could happen . . . worse.'

'I'm willing to take the risk. I haven't come straight from the convent, Felice.'

'No you haven't, Amy. But even if you did find him out there, you couldn't help him. More likely be a hindrance. Be patient and take a job here. It would be like old times.'

'No, Felice. If I was going to do that, I would have stayed in Mariposa. No, I want. . . .' Amy stopped talking as a large man with a shaggy salt-and-pepper beard suddenly appeared at their table. Beyond him, she glimpsed the clerk who was sidling back to the door that led through to the hotel.

'Miss Chard?' the big man inquired.

Amy looked up at the man. Experienced in such things, she noticed his bleak eyes. From a dark, ugly hole, his mouth twitched in what was intended to be a smile.

'What do you want, Garve?' It was Felice who spoke up.

Garve sniffed, pulled up a chair and sat down at the table. 'Are you lookin' for Wesley Teal?' he asked, his eyes on Amy.

'This is Grover Garve, Amy,' Felice continued to intercept. 'He used to be sheriff here, would you believe.'

Amy nodded at Garve. 'Do you know where he is?' she asked.

'Ha, I know where he's been all right,' Garve sneered. 'But he's done his time, an' I'm for lettin' bygones be bygones. Was it urgent, what you wanted him for?' the man pressed.

'If you know something, I'd appreciate you just saying it, without the questions, Mr Garve,' Amy told him.

'Yeah, that's right, Garve. Is he somewhere near here?' Felice joined in again.

Garve pulled at his beard and shook his head. 'No. He was, but he's gone. But if Miss Chard here wants to meet up with him, she could catch him in the gulch before he gets too far off. Otherwise she could be waitin' around here for days or weeks. You reckon on stayin' here for long, Miss Chard?'

'I haven't quite made up my mind yet. Even so, I'm not sure that you're the person I'd be telling, if I had.' Amy's tone was now frosty.

'Well, I'm just tryin' to help,' Garve said with a slow shrug. 'You see, I'm in the prospectin' business these days, an' I'll be goin' back to my camp first thing in the mornin'. Me an' my pard would be willin' to act as guides for you, if—'

This time Amy didn't need the interruption from Felice. 'Thank you, Mr Garve, she said. 'Your offer's a thoughtful one, but I won't be putting you to any trouble this time.'

Garve closed his gnarled fingers into a fist on the table. 'It ain't no trouble, Miss. But how do you know there's goin' to be a next time? Who's to say what happens out there? It's a dangerous place, where fellers have been known to just disappear.'

'I've said my piece, Mr Garve. And now I'd appreciate it if you left me and my friend alone,' Amy said sharply. 'Thank you, but no thank you.'

'Are you deaf as well as dumb, Garve?' Felice supported. 'She's never going to trail around any gulch diggings with you and that festering stinkbug you call your pard. Not even for a slice of the Gold Mountain itself.'

A snarl twisted Garve's face, his snaggled teeth showing through the gap in the front of his beard. 'You got too much to say, Felice,' he said. 'One o' these days someone's goin' to shut you up.'

'Well it won't be you, Garve. You're all finished as sheriff, remember?' Felice's tone was now openly scornful. 'Now you're just another crazy old gold-grubber.'

'I've a good mind to learn you some respect,' Garve's voice turned menacing and sharp.

'You've no mind left to be good with,' Felice snapped back. 'Now, clear off before I call for someone to throw you out on the street. You weren't invited to sit here.'

Amy involuntarily flinched, shrank back as Garve rose from his seat. There was a wild glitter in his eyes, and for a moment she thought he was going to slap out at Felice. But he turned and strode back towards the bar, saying something to a buckskin clad figure who was leaning on the counter.

'That's his partner,' Felice said, raising her chin and wrinkling her nose. 'Some say he's never taken a bath since his ma dropped him. Imagine turning your head on the pillow to see that close up?'

Amy smiled. 'I miss you, Felice,' she said reflectively. 'And it's a reason for staying in town. But that man's given me an idea. If I did have a guide – someone trustworthy – maybe I could go after Wesley.'

'Grover Garve's right about one thing, Amy. The gulch is a dangerous place, and you don't want to go out there. Not with him or anyone. Your man will come back. I know it.' Felice sighed. 'I wish I could meet the sort of man who made me feel that way,' she said, a trace of sadness veiling her face.

'Thank you, Felice,' Amy said firmly. 'I think you're beginning to understand.'

Felice didn't reply at once, then she nodded and smiled. 'Garve might be the hombre loco, but you could run for mujer loco,' she joked. 'Why don't you sleep on it? See how you feel tomorrow.'

'Tomorrow's just tomorrow. A day on, and I'll still

feel the same.' Amy looked around the big, smoke-filled room. 'If you don't know of anyone, I can mingle until. . . .'

'Yes, all right, Amy,' Felice conceded. 'There is a man. His name's Levi Norton, and he knows the gulch territory better than most. He's panned there himself for a few years. I'll find him for you.'

The jangling, tuneless music started up again, and the dour-faced man who had hired Felice returned from the bar.

'He wouldn't miss a dance if his feet were on fire,' Felice said from the cover of her hand. 'But he's harmless, and his dollars are as good as any one else's. I'll ask Levi to come over and talk to you.'

8

It was still dark when Amy rose next morning, dressing in the gear that Levi Norton had persuaded her to buy at the mercantile the night before. Armstrong Dove had opened up for them in response to Norton's insistence, and Amy came away from the store with a pair of jeans, a wool shirt, a sombrero and a pair of riding boots.

Out in the twilight of predawn on the deserted street, Amy made her way to the livery, her footsteps echoing on the pavement. She felt odd in her masculine outfit, but it was comfortable and allowed her to move freely.

Maybe I'll stick to them. Make Ma turn in her grave, she thought.

Norton was waiting at the livery with both horses saddled and ready. He was a leathery wisp of a man with a wide mouth and a pair of exceptional ears.

Old Mudfish, some called him. He was pushing sixty, and his face wore a grey stubble, but his movements had the springiness of a younger man.

The livery attendant was courteous and helpful. He took in Amy's appearance with palpable pleasure, helping her into the saddle.

'Danged if I know why you was doubtful about wearin' them duds,' Norton said and grinned. 'You look just fine.'

'Why thank you, Levi.' Amy smiled her appreciation. 'And thank you for what you're about to do.' She hadn't ridden much for a couple of years, but she'd always known how to handle horses. This one was a claybank filly, clear-footed and responsive to a light touch of the reins.

They rode together down Main, swung off to the north, towards the rearing rocks which bonded the gulch. It all looked picturesque from a distance, but appeared more unwelcoming as the two riders got closer. The new dawn brought a pink, fan-shaped tinge to the eastern sky, and then brighter light that shafted between the craggy masses of rock.

'Doesn't look like much could go wrong out here, Levi,' she said. 'It's a stunning land.'

'Yeah. Looks can be deceiving though, and fleeting.'

The long slope leading down into the gulch was a wide trail, used over the years by countless hopeful

66

gold-seekers in wagons, on horseback and on foot.

Amy was awed by the wilderness of fantastic, eroded rock. The hugeness of everything made her feel insignificant, a midget in a world of mighty grandeur. But when the gulch became a series of twisting valleys and creeks, something of her earlier hope and resolution faded. She was beginning now to see how her intention of going after Wesley Teal alone would have been such a bad and futile idea.

'Now I know what you all meant, Levi,' she conceded. 'It's handsome country, if not ideal for hunt-the-thimble.'

Norton twisted in his saddle and grinned across at her. 'And we've only just got going,' he said, jerking his thumb back the way they'd come, then pointing ahead. 'This is the main gulch we're in. It goes ahead for another twenty five miles, then it's rising foothills to the sierras. The way I figure, is to look for sign leading away from it. This rock floor won't tell us much, but there's soft ground ahead. We've got to be patient.'

'How do you know we're anywhere near the right place?' Amy asked.

'Austen Teal's gold was from a placer dig. So that cuts out the others, or most of them.'

'I see,' Amy replied after a moment, thinking she might have an idea of what Norton meant.

Shortly after midday, Norton called a halt where

one of the smaller valleys forked with the main gulch. A creek tumbled from the rocks to link with the main stream, flowing in a deeply eroded bed in the gulch. Amy built a fire, prepared a small meal from their provisions. Norton went prowling for sign, more than a mile away and out of sight on the other side of the gulch. He was gone a full hour, but when he returned, he looked satisfied.

'Looks like we're on the right trail,' he said, rubbing his leathery hands together. 'There's sign less than a day old, over on the west side. The land's hellish rough, but it's only a matter of being careful and taking our time. We'll ride there after chow.'

Norton's assertion that the ground was rough was no understatement. The gulch they rode into was on a lower level, and seepage from the slopes had brought down layers of earth as well as shale. It had eroded the hills and the upthrust rocks created fantastical shapes. At almost any point, a rider could happen on a mass of twisted rocks, be forced to make a long detour across ground that was either hard or near to quicksand.

But in other respects, the course was traversable. On some of the clear stretches, the sign was clearly visible, even to Amy. The possibility that it could be a rider other than Wesley Teal didn't occur to her, but she didn't say anything.

Norton, with an eye on Amy for signs of fatigue,

called another halt in the afternoon. Alongside a creek just off the main trail, there was tufts of bunch grass for the horses and a stand of desert willow for cover.

Thirty minutes later, the sound of hoofbeats echoed across the gulch as Amy and Norton sipped steaming coffee. Norton was quick to his feet, peering across the tumble of rocks and upthrusts.

Now, Amy spoke up. 'Do you think it's Wesley?' she asked, hopefully.

Norton listened more intently to the hoofbeats that were coming from the far side of the gulch, waiting until he was sure they were headed towards them. 'Not unless he doubled back,' he growled. 'This hombre's behind us. Young Teal wouldn't be.' He glared at the fire. 'Must have seen the smoke. Guess I'm getting old,' he added. He shook his head and unflipped his holster, drew his old walnut-handled revolver.

Amy took a glance around, pensively placed her coffee on the ground in front of her. There was enough cover, but as luck would have it, no way out, no escape without being seen by the oncoming rider.

'There's some devilish beings roam these parts,' Norton muttered. 'And, unless I'm mistaken, god-damnit, this one's Grover Garve,' he cursed.

Between rocky upthrusts, the rider had come into view briefly, but was now out of sight again. Norton waited, his thumb clicking back the hammer, setting the action of his revolver.

Garve dragged on his reins a few yards from the small encampment. 'You good folk been expectin' me,' he called out.

'Might've blown your head off, if so,' Norton rasped. 'Are you trailing us?' he demanded harshly.

Garve shook his head. He dismounted and walked towards the pair, his eye on the gun in Norton's fist. 'This is where I work, Mudfish,' he said with a laugh. 'Didn't you know?'

'Yeah, I knew. But it ain't right here, so what do you want, Garve?'

'Put that cannon down and I'll tell you,' Garve said. 'I saw your smoke a while back an' figured some pilgrims might be tryin' out this part. But as it is, can't a man pay a friendly call?' He looked at Amy. 'See you got yourself a guide after all, Miss?'

'That's right,' Norton snapped. 'So we don't need any help from you.'

Garve had stopped half a dozen paces from the bristling old-timer. 'What's got you so snuffy?'

'Your claim's two miles back. What are you doing this far up the gulch?'

'Ain't much of a claim. A little pay dirt to keep us in coffee and crackers, that's all. I'm looking for something better,' Garve said.

'Yeah, like Austen Teal's claim,' Norton countered.

70

'Listen, Garve. Wesley Teal's back, and none of us know if he's going catch up with his old man's gold. But what I do know is, it certainly ain't going to be you. So get going while you can. I got a short way with jumpers.'

Amy watched Garve with increasing unease. Having developed a sense for ulterior motives in the man, she disliked and distrusted him, thought he was keeping Norton talking for a purpose, when he could and should have moved on. She looked beyond Garve, up and further along the gulch in the direction he'd ridden from.

Garve was talking again, but now in a more appeasing tone. But Amy didn't hear his words. She was too intent on picking up another sound, recalling Garve's partner, the unsavoury-looking man in grimed buckskins.

Coldness touched her feelings, and she shivered when she thought she saw movement around the standing rocks. She saw that Norton had heard it too, saw his fist tighten around the butt of his gun.

'There's someone else out there, Levi,' she yelled. 'Be careful.'

The gunshot exploded into her words, booming and echoing madly around the rocky terrain. Amy screamed involuntarily against the sound, again when she saw Norton's body lurch forward from the impact of the bullet. Norton gasped, swung around and fired twice from his old Colt, before sagging to his knees. He looked back at Amy and mouthed, 'sorry'. Then, coldly and deliberately, Garve shot him between the shoulder blades.

9

'You scum! You murderous scum!' Amy's fear was flooded by fury as she looked up from the crumpled body of Levi Norton. She made a sudden dash towards Norton's old Colt, but Garve was too quick. He strode forward, kicking the weapon clear of Amy's grasping hand.

'Stick to what you do best,' he snarled. 'You'll live a smut longer.'

'Why did you have to kill him?' Amy choked out. Then, before Garve responded, she heard the sounds again, but this time a nauseating, feral smell assailed her. She gasped, turned quickly to see the lanky man in a dirty skin outfit who she'd seen across the bar room in Mariposa. He was well over six feet tall and wore a slouch hat. His face was mostly covered by a yellowish-grey moustache and beard.

'You can smell him from five miles, so he ain't ever going

73

to surprise you,' Felice had said with a crude wink.

But she was wrong. Beaver John stole up on Amy quiet as a stalkin' cat. With tawny narrowed eyes, the man stood looking down at her, grinning with quid-stained teeth. 'Better'n wrappin' yourself in a saddle mat, eh Grover?' he called out.

Amy shrank away from the man as his eyes ran over her body, even moved closer to Garve. The ex-lawman was a murderous brute, but Amy knew she was his means to an end. Garve's sole interest was in getting his hands on Teal's gold.

'How much did Teal tell you about the gold?' Garve asked her.

'Nothing. I didn't know much about anything until I reached Calido Run,' Amy said.

'You expect me to believe that? You're chasin' him through hell's half acre, just to be around when he makes his find. You're stretchin' the blanket there, lady.'

'I know about it now, because it was what most everyone in town was talking about,' Amy answered back. 'But Wesley hadn't spoken to me about any gold strike.'

'Hmm. An' now you do know, you want your share. Is that it?'

Amy clenched her hands. 'It's Wesley I want. I wanted him before I knew about any gold. I doubt that's ever been said about the likes of you.'

Beaver John gave a cackling laugh, and surprisingly, Garve grinned. Then he nodded, his expression more cunning.

'I've had my moments,' he said slowly. 'So, if you're talkin' straight, I figure Teal told you as much as he told everyone else ... nothin'. Trusted you about the same.'

Amy stayed silent while Garve went on. 'But on the other hand, maybe he didn't tell you so's to keep you out o' trouble. Maybe you're just as important to him as his pa's gold.'

'Again, that's something which I doubt you have any experience of. I'm surprised you even thought of it,' Amy sniped back.

'Yeah, well like I said. Fact is, a man can pick up a good-lookin' girl, most anywhere. Hotels an' dog holes are full of 'em. But can the same man pick up a fortune in gold as easy?' Garve presented Beaver John with a warning scowl. 'You hear that, John? She's our ticket to Teal's gold. So I don't want her clipped, you understand?'

'Yeah, I understand,' Beaver John grunted sourly.

Amy remembered something else that her friend Felice had said, and she nearly smiled with relief.

Garve saw the look across Amy's face. 'But I'll change my mind, if you don't answer my questions,' he said. 'He'll make you a sorry looking gift for the young Wesley Teal.'

Amy nodded dumbly.

'How come ol' Mudfish took a ride on this side of the gulch?' Garve continued. 'Did he pick up anythin' around here?'

Amy stared ahead belligerently and didn't answer.

Garve took her shoulder in a firm grip. 'You really want John to exchange his ol' fiddle-head for you?' he threatened. 'If Teal's left sign, we'll find it all right, but you'll save us time.'

'No need, Grove,' Beaver John chipped in. 'I seen it when I come circlin' around. Some of it's as good as lookin' in a picture book.'

'Good. That means the lode's probably up one of the creeks comin' in from this side,' Garve said, the greedy gleam in his eyes again. 'I been waitin' five years for this, so let's make a move. You go on ahead, an' I'll take ol' Mudfish's horse as a pack pony. Gold's a real heavy provision.' he added with a wicked grin.

Amy looked down at the still body of Levi Norton. She felt a sudden choke and tears welled in her eyes. Where she was and what she was doing suddenly seemed so cheap and meaningless. Levi had simply tried to help her, and he'd died for it with an apology.

'What are you going to do about Levi?' she asked suppressing her anger. 'You can't leave him here like this.'

'Well, from the look of him, he ain't goin' to mind.

An' they sure ain't,' he rasped, stabbing his finger skywards.

Amy looked up, shuddered at the sight of a lone vulture floating slowly in a circle directly above them.

'He knows when there's pickin's. Him an' me both,' Garve said and took Amy's arm. He gave her a shove towards her horse, standing beside her while she mounted. He looped the reins of Norton's horse over his arm before climbing into his own saddle.

'Reckon Norton was on the right track,' Beaver John claimed excitedly as Amy and Garve rode along-side. 'There's sign here as fresh as paint, headed straight for the place, I'll bet.'

The trio moved on slowly. Occasionally, Beaver John lost the sign, picking it up again where softer ground appeared. He was becoming more and more elated, chuckling to himself, dribbling tobacco juice at the thought of returning to town a rich man, someone of celebrity and significance.

Garve on the other hand was tense, glaring impa-tiently each time Beaver John called a halt to look for lost sign. Beaver John was taking nothing for granted. The man they were searching for could have taken any one of the many rifts, creeks and narrow valleys which they'd ridden past. And it still held good for all the other small cut-offs that lay ahead.

The gulch floor lifted further on, rising between

gnarled, weather-beaten rocks. There was only a narrow trail, and it was on this higher level that Beaver John suddenly stopped. He shouted for Garve, who was some distance behind him and on a lower level.

'What's the goddamn fuss?' Garve said as he reigned in ahead of Amy.

Beaver John was staring across to the other side of the gulch. 'There's three of 'em,' he said. 'They've been with us a while.'

Trailing the smell, probably, Amy thought immediately, but didn't say.

Garve cursed and swung his horse around, rode from the sightline of the oncoming riders. 'Who the hell are they? You recognize any of 'em?' he demanded.

'No, still too far away,' Beaver John growled, his tawny eyes glittering angrily.

Garve looked quickly to Amy. 'Was Teal fixin' to meet up with anyone here?' he rasped.

'I already told you, I never knew where *here* was,' Amy answered, despair beginning to strain her voice.

'Oh, you know all right, I can see by your face.'

'There were three men in Mariposa. But I'm pretty sure Wesley wasn't going to meet up with them anywhere else.'

'Why? Who the hell were they?' Garve persisted as the hoofbeats echoed closer through the gulch

'Would they know about the gold? Answer me quick, girl.'

'They had a fight with Wesley. So yes, maybe they do.'

'What do you know about these men?'

'One of them's called Korne. And that's all I know,' Amy replied wearily.

'Farley Korne.' Garve repeated the name, twisting it around anxiously in his mouth. Korne was the man who'd stepped into the shoes of Ike Whittman when Wesley Teal had shot and killed him. Garve didn't need to be told the names of the other two. The trio were still a team, and now after five years it looked like they too had their eye on the trail to Teal's gold.

'If what the girl said was true, them fellers weren't short in the town,' Beaver John said.

Garve nodded. 'Yeah, waitin' for the one person who could lead 'em to the goddamn mother lode,' he agreed.

Beaver John uttered a guttural sound, hawked and spat. 'Hope this don't mean we'll be shootin' it out with 'em.'

'Hell no. They're all gun sharks. I'd best go head 'em off . . . try an' talk to 'em,' Garve decided. 'An' get the girl out o' the way. If they know about her, they'll be askin' goddamn awkward questions. There's dozens of cutbank holes around here, maybe a big bear's den. Put her in one, an' make sure she's hogged down proper.'

Amy clenched her hands. 'I'm not going anywhere with you,' she hissed at seeing Beaver John's malignant grin.

'Oh, yes you are, missy,' Beaver John snarled, stepping up and laying a hand on her arm. 'An' keep your mouth shut, else you'll find somethin' stuffed in it.'

Amy wanted to yell. But knowing she'd be no better off with the incoming riders than with these two, she checked, allowing Beaver John to lead her horse into the gully.

'Show yourself, mister,' Farley Korne shouted, his cold flat voice resonating through the twisted rock forms.

Garve cursed fearfully, sent his horse up the slope until he was above the three riders on the lower level. He pulled his Colt, but was only thinking of using it as a last resort. 'Hell's teeth, you remind me o' Farley Korne,' he shouted, his voice speciously cheerful. 'Didn't know you an' your pards were around Calido Run.' As a token of peaceable intention, he pushed his gun back into leather. 'It's been a few moons, Farley.'

'We're comin' up,' Korne called out. 'So leave your gun where you just put it.'

Garve looked down and across to the close wall of

the gulch. Amy and her horse were out of sight, but Beaver John was coming up towards him at a lope, and he cursed again with relief. In the few minutes it took for Korne and the other two to find their way to the rising slope between the rocks, Beaver John was back and standing beside his horse.

'She's OK, Grove,' he muttered. 'A real little cow bunny, that one.'

The two men eyed the hawk-nosed Farley Korne who was leading the way ahead of the big Jack Bass and the pale-eyed Mose Parker.

'You're still as rank, John,' Korne said, grimacing with a half turn away. 'I should've remembered to stay up wind.'

Beaver John growled something deep in his throat, and his eyes gleamed vindictively. 'Yeah, perhaps you should've,' he replied cautiously, gunplay not being one of the things he was too proficient at.

'You met up with Wesley Teal, Grover?' Korne then asked of Garve.

Garve shook his head. 'No, but I heard he was in town,' he said uneasily.

'I'm not talkin' about town, an' you know it,' Korne retorted, his eyes firmly fixed on the ex-lawman. 'He's out here somewhere, an' that's what you're doin'.'

'I'm here because our work's here,' Garve corrected.

'We got claims, John an' me.'

'Yeah? An' just where the hell are they, exactly?'

'There's a couple behind, an' a couple more ahead.'

Korne laughed. 'Yeah funny. You're huntin' Wesley Teal,' he said in a more abrupt manner. 'But you figure he knows just where his old man's lode is. That's the truth of it.'

Garve shook his head. 'Listen, Farley,' he said. 'Me an' John's been under an' over every place where there's likely placer diggings. So I got me a big doubt over ol' Teal ever gettin' anythin' more'n some goddamn orphan nuggets.'

'Hmm, maybe,' Korne said doubtfully. 'An' you ain't seen any sign o' the young Wesley?'

'I already told you no, Farley. See, I'm figurin' one o' the new claims is goin' to pan out. It ain't chasin', it's here now, I can smell it. Mind you, if I do run across any sign I think's his, I'll probably tag along for the hell of it.'

Korne watched the sweat bead across Garve's darkly skinned forehead. 'Could bring a heap o' trouble down on you, Grover,' he said, the flat inflection of his voice intensifying the threat.

Garve smiled weakly. 'They call it fool's gold, Farley. We both know that. It's chasin' down a million to one chance.'

'Yeah, well we've got other business with Wesley

Teal,' Korne said. 'Me an' the boys don't aim to have anyone gettin' in the way of it. That includes pokin' their noses where they shouldn't. You understand?'

'Yeah, I understand, Farley. You don't want me an' John around.' The ex-lawman's eyes were baleful, cursing long and hard after Korne and the other two wheeled their horses away.

Farley Korne drew rein on the lower level, out of sight of Garve and Beaver John. 'I wonder what the hell they're after?' he said, thoughtfully looking to the sky as three buzzards circled in a long, descending swoop. Then he looked at the two other riders. 'Did you see the spare horse?' he asked them.

'Yeah. I sort o' figured you was goin' to ask him about it,' Mose Parker said.

Korne shook his head. 'No. If it was Teal's horse, he'd o' lied. There's another way to find out,' he replied, with a sly grin.

'Could be they got rid of him soon as they spotted us,' Parker suggested.

Korne fixed his eyes on the rock wall close by, calculating the terrain around them. 'We'll know soon enough,' he said. 'If they've got him holed up, they're not goin' to make a move towards him until they're sure we're out o' the gulch,' he said. 'So, let's take a look around, an' keep your eyes open. If there is a hidey-hole, it won't be too far off the beaten track.'

Hugging the rock wall, Korne led the way along the lower level. He stopped once, frowning when he briefly glimpsed Beaver John and Garve riding between tall-standing rock piles. But they were riding away. *Of course you are. You know I'm watchin'*, he thought, his eyes narrowing in deliberation. *But if Teal's here somewhere, you'll be back.*

10

Amy lay forlornly in a dry, deserted bear den, her horse tied-in to a wedge of nearby rock. Beaver John had used a couple of rawhide strings he carried about him to lash her ankles and wrists together, gagging her with her own cotton wipe. For five, maybe ten minutes after he'd gone, Amy had writhed and strained against the bonds. But she had to give up, collapsing sore and exhausted to the shale strewn floor.

Grover Garve had said she was trade goods for the whereabouts of Austen Teal's gold strike. But Amy knew that in the unlikely event of Wesley accepting the bargain, Garve wouldn't. Another witness would be too risky. Opportunely for him, man or woman could simply disappear in this rocky wilderness and never be found.

After what seemed an interminable time, she heard her horse nicker, then moments later, the slow clop of hoofs. And there were distant voices, muffled and unrecognizable. The filly whinnied softly, but the sounds of the riders didn't carry any further. As the slow hoofbeats lessened and died away, she tried again to loosen her bonds. Against the sharp, biting pain, she felt a slight loosening of the thongs around her wrists and increased her struggle.

The voices returned, but the sound was now of iron-shod hoofs on hard rock and it was mingled with footsteps. The men were leading their horses, and Amy realized it wasn't Garve and his partner. It had to be the three men they'd seen riding across from the other side of the gulch.

From what little she knew of the men back in Mariposa, Amy guessed there would be no advantage in getting freed by them. They would likely use her just as ruthlessly as Garve. But the voices were much closer now, and her horse's uneasy whinny got an answer.

'Stay right where you are, Mo. An' remember we got no friends,' came the voice of Farley Korne.

Amy saw the shadow of a man appear at the entrance to the bear den, another, bigger silhouette showing behind him.

'Well, well, reckon we might have got ourselves a

Teal,' Korne said. With Bass following, the man walked slowly into the gloomy cavern, grunting in surprise when he saw Amy glaring up at him.

'Goddamn. Look what daddy bear's dragged in,' he rasped, stepping towards Amy. He leaned down and, holding her by the arms, lifted her to her feet. He released her arms, took the gag from her mouth, and untied her ankles.

Amy was unable to keep the fear from her voice as she eyed Korne and the big, scar-faced, half-breed. 'They were forcing me to go with them. When they saw you coming, they put me in here,' she said meekly, and rubbed her mouth with the back of her hand. 'I just want to go back to Calido Run. I think I can find my way alone.' Amy knew that asking for help against a common rival will sometimes elicit support, if only short term.

But Korne wasn't ready to fall for it. 'Steady on, sister,' he said. 'It ain't usual to have a woman in tow. So why were you?' He eyed Amy closely. 'I've seen you somewhere. Mariposa, I reckon?'

'Yes, I came from there.'

'Same place that Wesley Teal came from. Are you his girl?'

'No of course I'm not,' Amy protested. 'I worked at Sappers Hole, which is where you probably saw me. I'm nobody's girl but the best payer. You must know that.'

'Yeah. He comes ridin' into Calido Run, an' then you come ridin' into Calido Run,' Korne said drily. 'Mighty happenstance or what?'

'If you leave Mariposa for any reason, you'll probably end up here. My friend did,' Amy replied quickly. 'I came to work.'

'What at? Pannin' for gold?' Korne said, and coughed out a harsh laugh. 'That still don't explain what you're doin' with Grover Garve.'

Amy bit her lip, decided it best to come up with a part truth. 'I did get to know Wesley Teal,' she admitted in a low voice. 'But I didn't want everyone to know, and I did come here to get a job. That's why I went to the Picture Paint Saloon. My friend's name is Felice.'

'An' Teal?'

'I knew he was here, yes. Why is that so. . . .'

A shout from outside broke up Amy's reply, was followed by the echoing boom of a Colt and the sharp sound of a bullet smacking into rock, close by.

'Farley, they're back,' Mose Parker called out a second later, his gun roaring almost immediately.

Korne uttered a curse and ran from the cavern with Bass.

Amy, seeing her opportunity, immediately followed to the den's entrance. From higher in the rocks, Beaver John fired a quick shot down at Parker.

Then another explosion from further along, revealed the cover from where Garve was shooting.

'Get behind 'em,' Korne snarled at Parker. 'We'll hold 'em from here. Go on – move.' He loosed off two quick shots as a bullet crushed against the rock wall inches from his head. He flung himself to the ground, crawling to the low protection of an outcrop about a dozen yards ahead.

Bass was already in cover, squeezed in close to the rock wall. His gun was roaring, targeting up towards Garve.

Beaver John showed again, but from up above where there was more cover. He moved about to confuse the gunmen below, but he wasn't allowing himself time to pinpoint either of the men who were his targets, and his bullets were mostly wide and wasted.

Amy stood terrified and ashen-faced, flinching back from the opening of the den. The guns were blasting and echoing incessantly around her, bullets whining past. For the moment, none of the protagonists had a thought for her. If she could make it through the gap between the rock wall and the uprearing rocks, without being seen or getting hit, it was her chance for her to escape.

She looked back desperately at her horse, shared it's sentiment of frozen horror. Even if she escaped a ricocheting bullet, there was a good chance of the filly being shot. 'Sorry,' she muttered. 'What have

89

you done to deserve all this?'

Amy stepped from the shadow of the cavern, removed the horse's reins from the wedge of rock, and, holding its head in close, turned it back towards the den's entrance. With its ears flattened and it's eyes bulging with fear, it snorted at the continued uproar of he guns. 'You're doing fine. And now we're riding away. Trust me,' Amy said quietly.

Then Korne's voice echoed loudly. 'Mo's got him from behind,' he yelled. 'That's one of 'em down. Don't let Garve escape.'

Garve's Colt was still blasting. But the sound was losing its volume as the ex-lawman shifted his position. Garve knew he was now fighting three gunmen alone, was trying desperately to get back to where he'd left his horse. Korne and Bass were equally intent on stopping him, and they moved forward now, hugging the rock walls, no longer staying in cover. Further ahead and over on the side, Mose Parker was shooting in at an angle.

'Keep it up, Mo,' Korne yelled out. 'He's corralled . . . got no chance.'

Amy felt a surge of hope. For the moment she was forgotten, so, issuing calming noises, she led the filly off. The gunmen were out of sight now, around a turn in the rock face. Although an occasional bullet droned wildly overhead, there was no imminent danger and she climbed into the saddle. Needing little encouragement to get away, she leaned forward and smacked the filly's neck, swinging them off and away from the shooting.

11

Wesley Teal drew rein, sat his saddle and eased his Stetson from the sweat ridge in his forehead. He was looking at a gap in the rock wall on the western side of the gulch. The breach led away in two directions, two creeks running down from two valleys to join at the gulch. The swollen, combined creek coursed across the gulch in a twisting swift stream between rugged upthrusts, finding a level over on the eastern side of the gulch further down. Wesley was deep in thought, waiting and wanting to recall something that had been lost in time, and after five minutes, it came to him.

When he was a kid, the family had driven their trail wagon through Snake Pass on their way to the New Mexico border. From then on, his pa often made up names for places and things, if they featured something else. More often than not, he'd used Spanish, said that considering where they were headed, it was fine learning.

And now there it was in front of him. Without knowing it, it was why he'd stopped. The configuration of water courses was Slingshot Creek. It was also a creation of Austen Teal, and Wesley felt a thump of excitement in his chest. Slingshot Creek was where he was supposed to start from, he was certain of that. But where and what did his pa mean by Tortola Rocks? A moment later, his mind was playing with an idea, and he nearly smiled. Eager now, Wesley sent his horse into the swift-flowing water. When the animal finally got a foothold on the far side, they were on the soft verge of the southern arm of the creek.

The valley that Wesley rode into was narrow. Its rock-strewn sides crowded in darkly, and irregular slopes rose from the valley floor to a shelving outcrop running parallel to the barren rocks below. Above that, timber stands underpinned the brighter skyline. He started along the winding valley, the late sun glistening on the rock wall alongside the creek.

There were many steps of rock that made natural weirs, any one of which could have been the barrier for alluvial deposits. But Wesley was after one in particular, the one with the magical bedding contours that trapped and held grains of gold.

Eventually, the snaking valley narrowed. The rocks

lessened and sloping land, tree-clad and grassy, took their place. Wesley had reached the limit of the rock-bound wall on the southern arm. So, if his understanding of his father's dying words had been right, he'd missed the place called Tortola Rocks.

He turned his horse. His own impatience troubled him, but he forced himself to use his imagination on every shape, every form created by light and shadow. He dismounted and hunkered down, looked closely at rock formations that melded with water races and shallow steps. 'Come on, show yourself,' he muttered. 'I'm too tired for goddamn games.'

The sun was lower, throwing long slanting rays across the twisting valley. Wesley moved slowly, his eyes ever searching, sweeping the land ahead.He peered along the creek and saw a weir, a drop which took only part of the creek water, the rest coursing away down a rugged slope.The waterfall itself was a mere rope of water, but in the wet season would make an impressive torrent.

He reined in where part of the creek widened to form a small lagoon. Then he stared, mesmerized at the slanting sunlight playing across the water, cursing with mild amazement at the shapes being created along the edge of the lake. 'That's what I've been looking for, Pa. The turtles. Fooled 'em all except me,' he muttered. The short line of dark glistening, humpy-back rocks broke from his imagination, and the words escaped as a loud exclamation. 'Tortola Rocks!'

It was all there, the low cascade which would become torrential in season, a potential site for alluvial gold to collect in the gouged out scrape that must lie at the foot of the shallow weir. But it was small wonder that any man who had prowled the gulch over the past five years hadn't been able to unearth Austen Teal's secret, and that included Grover Garve. Even Wesley, with his special visual clue could have passed it by if it hadn't been for the low, accenting rays of the sun.

'Reckon I might've got his sidekick,' Mose Parker called out hopefully.

'Yeah? Well, either way, Garve's high-tailed back to Calido Run,' Farley Korne growled, his face pulling into a heavy scowl. 'Teal's gold will be enough for half the town to line up solid behind him.'

'Huh. I don't reckon he's likely to want anyone sharin' in a gold strike,' Parker suggested.

'No. But the crazy ol' coot would a sight sooner do that than let us get away with it,' Korne snorted back. 'Hell, the girl,' he said, suddenly and banged his fist against his thigh.

A few minutes later, when Bass and Parker caught up with him, Korne was staring into the empty cavern. 'You check for sign. Any goddamn sign,' he snapped breathlessly at Bass after making a long string of vengeful curses.

The three men mounted and Bass led the way back. The sign took them over to the far side of the gulch, where it disappeared from the rock floor.

Bass shrugged. 'If she ain't headed back, we'll pick up sign over on the other side, along with Teal's,' he said.

'Goddamn Grover Garve,' Korne muttered. 'The girl could've been our trump.'

'It's still three cards against one,' Parker said, slapping his gun butt.

They headed across to the other side of the gulch where Bass found sign. But like Korne had said, it was an indication that Garve had headed back across to the far side of the gulch, and on to Calido Run.

'We don't have much time,' Korne grated. 'Garve ain't goin' to walk out a broken man, just leavin' us to grab what he's been after for years. An' this goddamn girl could start somethin' if she decides to go visit the sheriff. He's a different sort o' lawman to what Grover Garve was.'

'Huh. *Most* lawmen are that, Farley,' Parker agreed. 'We've likely got two piles o' trouble stacked against us.'

Fifteen minutes later, Bass grunted with satisfaction when he picked up sign. It wasn't recent enough to be from either Garve's or Amy's horse, so had to be Teal's.

At the place known to Wes Teal as Slingshot Creek, they lost the trail along the softer ground of the bank edges.

'This must be it,' Korne said, his eyes now glinting with anticipation. 'Let's get across.'

They rode across the creek and within minutes of reaching the other side there was clear sign heading along the south arm.

'Looks to me like a feller who's got some idea where he's headed,' Korne said thoughtfully.

They rounded a sharp crook in the valley which immediately doubled back. Bass's attention was fixed on the ground, so it was Korne's restless eyes probing the shadowed valley that spotted the distant horse and rider moving along slowly ahead of them.

'There he is. Hold up,' he grated. It was too far to pick out the identity of the rider, but the overall size was near enough for Korne. 'Wesley Teal,' he said quietly. 'It's you, goddamnit.'

Keeping to the shadows and using the contours of the land for cover, Korne moved them up on the lone rider. Shortly, the man they had been following turned his horse and drew rein. They watched him sit his saddle for a while, gazing across a stretch of pooling water into which a column of water tumbled.

Korne made a quick assessment of the landscape around them. It wasn't part of his plan to stage a gunfight, with the chance of Teal getting killed accidentally or otherwise. Right now, with what looked like Teal getting close to uncovering the site of his father's gold, Korne reckoned the best time for Teal to get shot would be after he'd offered up his information, not before.

On the far side of the creek where Teal sat his horse was a fairly wide stretch of level ground up to the base of a sheer rock face, but opposite where the three riders had halted, there were some good hand and foot-holds.

'Get yourself up there, Mo,' Kern said, pointing across the creek.

'Where? What the hell for?'

'The higher ground. You can swing a loop at him.'

'Jesus, Farley, I ain't no goddamn roper,' he grunted. 'Maybe I could drop a catch on him if he don't take his mind off whatever it is that's got him so occupied. But if he spots me up there with no cover, I'm dead meat. There's no lasso invented yet that beats a goddamn bullet.'

'Just keep quiet an' wait your time,' Korne snapped. 'Think o' the worth of what you're ropin' in. We'll be movin' down slow, an' we'll have him covered. Remember, dead men don't talk. So no shootin'.'

Parker grumbled doubtfully as he sent his horse across the creek. A few minutes later he dismounted, and, with a coil of rope around his shoulder, started his climb up the rocks. Korne watched him until he reached the top, nodded at Bass and sent his horse at a slow walk towards the motionless rider.

12

Wesley Teal had sat on his horse for some minutes taking in the reach of the place only he knew as Tortola Rocks. The cascade of water tumbled into a small circle of foam, indicating flat bed-rock in the shallows beneath. If there were deposits of gold, the rock would extend only a short distance before breaking off in a shelf. There was little doubt that Austen Teal's distinctive observation had alerted him of the strike.

Wesley sent his horse into the shallow stretch of crystal clear water, and then in a half circle around the base of the cascade. He could clearly see where the rock ended close to the far side of the creek, the narrow strip of gravel between the rock and dry land. The excitement gripped him as he envisioned what was beneath it, an expressive smile crossed his face when he thought of having someone to tell of his find.

They were standing in a foot of water when he saw the forward flick of his horse's ears. 'Yeah, I know, we've got company,' he said softly. He twisted in his saddle, looked up sharply, but didn't avoid the lariat which came snaking down in a wide loop. He felt the sudden grasp of the rope around his arms and body, made an effort to free his imprisoned arms, but it was too late and he was dragged clear of his saddle. The next moment he was floundering in the shallows, his horse plunging across to the stretch of dry land below the rocks.

He heard the thump of hoofs, saw two riders coming towards him at a gallop. He made a grab for his Colt, but could only offer a helpless curse when a gun roared and a bullet spat into the water alongside him.

'Leave it, Wes. I might not miss next time,' Farley Korne yelled out.

Immediately, the rope tightened, and Wesley was dragged towards the bank in an awkward tripping run through the shallow water. Korne and Bass were riding through the creek towards him. Korne, his hawkish face distorted by a grin of savage triumph, leapt from his saddle on the verge of the creek as Wesley's feet made the dry ground. The man whipped Wesley's gun from its holster, lobbed it behind him back into the pool.

'OK Mo, slacken off,' he commanded Parker.

101

The lariat became loose and Wesley spread his arms. The loop dropped, and with his eyes locked on Korne, he stepped clear, rubbing at the forearm flesh where the rope had bitten.

'Get yourself over there, Wes,' Korne said, the look in his eyes making false the hard grin across his mouth.

Wesley walked slowly up on to the dry, gravelled stretch towards the cliffs which formed a high cutbank.

'Good work, Mo,' Korne said, as Mose Parker scrambled back down the cliffside. 'Somethin' to bear in mind if your trigger finger cracks up.' But Korne wasn't looking at his stocky sidekick, he was prudently returning the challenge of Wesley's glare. 'Looks like your bonanza days are over, Wes,' he rasped. 'Tell us what you know, and I'll make sure you've a pot to piss in.'

Wesley looked into Korne's chilling eyes. He smiled grimly, wanting to tell the man that parts of your life really can flash before you. 'I know what it is you're talking about, Korne, and you're very generous. But I haven't found the gold. Not yet, anyways,' he said and shrugged.

'We're none of us fools, Wes. We know you ain't found it yet,' Korne snapped in response. 'But you know where to start lookin'.'

'Do you think I'd be standing here, cooling my

heels, staring around me, if I knew that? I'd have gone straight there, goddamnit.'

Korne surveyed the spot slowly, critically. 'I think you're bluffin',' he said with a wry grin. 'I think you're found it already. Maybe it's right here.'

Wesley looked around him. 'Just goes to show how little you boys know about gold deposits,' he said, keeping the tone of his voice indifferent. 'I only figured on making night camp in the lee of the rock. But if you reckon it's pay dirt, why don't you dig around some? There's a shovel hitched to my saddle, and it'll save me the trouble. Go ahead. I doubt you'll be the first who's tried,' he added coolly.

As if considering the idea, Korne looked to where Wesley's horse had stopped its first spooked run.

More than ready to hand out punishment, Bass was glaring at the prisoner. 'Quit the chaff, Farley,' he snarled angrily. 'The whole territory knows his ol' man told him the landmarks. Now he can tell us. Let me show you how.'

'You hear that, Wes?' Korne asked in his toneless voice. 'Back in Mariposa, you put some lead into his leg, an' understandably he's still sore about it. You really don't want me to set him on to you. Him an' them cruel Apache tortures.'

'I can't tell you what I don't know.'

'Just tell me what your pa said. I'll decide on the value of it.'

103

Wesley hesitated. If he could play for time, lead the three of them on with patchy information, a chance might come up for him. It didn't matter how slim the chance was because at the moment he didn't have much to lose. But after he told them where the lode was likely to be found, and once they'd got sight of gold they'd be in fever and he'd be a dead man. *Probably end up shooting each other,* he thought.

Wesley sighed, dropped his shoulders. 'He told me to find a place called Aqua Hendido,' he lied. 'Why's a long story. But that's what he said, all he said. I figured I was riding it.'

Korne nodded, his expression almost cordial. 'Yeah, well maybe he did. But a lot of men could spend months, maybe years pokin' an' diggin' along here, even if they chose the right fork. So, your old man would've coughed up a tad more'n that, Wes.'

'He didn't have time to say any more, because he was dying with Ike Wittman's bullet in him,' Wesley explained icily. 'He could have muttered something about a place called Tortola, but there's nowhere within a hundred miles called anything like that.'

Korne let out a long, exasperated breath.He stepped closer to Wesley and lashed out with a bony hand, smacking it across his prisoner's mouth. 'You're lying. For the last time, goddamnit, tell us everythin',' he muttered.

Wesley lurched backwards, the taste of blood in his

mouth. He was still staggering when Bass, on one side of him, joined in. Struck again, he went to ground with a blow to the jaw. Bass's boot swung viciously and slammed into Wesley's ribs, driving the air from his lungs and sending pain lancing through his body.

'For chris'sake, if I made something up, you might turn *real* nasty,' he seethed, rolling away as Bass raised his foot again.

Quickly, Korne reached out and gripped Bass by the arm. 'Hold it,' he snapped. 'Get up, Wes. Tell us, before he gets mad,' he added harshly.

Wesley rose slowly to his feet. Wiping blood from his chin with the back of his hand, he was gasping because of the pain across his ribs and chest.

'Less than a minute, I'll have him squealin' like a stuck pig,' Bass snarled, limping closer to Wesley.

Korne looked hard at the dark, scarred face of the half-breed and shook his head. 'No. I don't think you're goin' to beat it out of him.' He then turned to Mose Parker. 'Get your rope ready again,' he said. 'We've got to be more subtle.'

Wondering precisely what Korne had in mind, Wesley swallowed hard as the stumpy man obeyed.

13

'OK, loop one end around his right arm,' Korne told Parker.

Parker slipped a noose over Wesley's arm, grinning as he pulled tight.

'Good,' Korne said. 'Do the same to his left, but use the other end. Jack, you bring up the horses.'

A combination of panic, and an idea of what was about to happen galvanized Wesley into action. He lashed out with his foot, caught Parker on the knee, and the man's leg collapsed under him. Wesley whirled away, and dived at Korne's legs. Korne's gun roared as Wesley twisted and reached up, but Bass was already lunging forward, grasping for the rope that trailed from Wesley's right arm. The next moment, Wesley felt his arm being jerked from its socket, his outstretched fingers grabbing air as he went sprawling to the ground.

Korne pounced into a semi-crouch, his fist pounding down into Wesley's jaw. Half-stunned, Wesley had his left arm gripped tight and pinned against the ground. The free end of the rope was looped back over his arm, and yanked hard.

'Now cut it,' Korne said roughly. Bass drew his knife and slashed down at where Korne indicated, leaving Wesley with a trailing rope on each arm.

What the hell are they going to do? Wesley speculated fearfully, expecting another part of his life to flash before him.

Korne gestured to Bass. 'Get him up, an' fasten these ends to the saddle horns. An' watch him.'

Wesley stood there shakily as the horses were brought up either side of him and Bass fastened the ends of the ropes to the saddle horns.

'OK Wes, I'm givin' you a last chance,' Korne said. 'You ain't like the rest of them sourdoughs, pokin' an' scrabblin' in the dirt. So just tell me where your old man made his find.'

Wesley shook his head. 'How many more times? You know as much as me.'

'I really didn't want to have to drag the truth from you, Wes. But you give me no choice.' Korne stepped across to his own horse, pulled himself into the saddle. 'Mo, get yourself up into that saddle,' he directed.

The two horses moved slightly under the prompt

107

of a spur, and Wesley's arms were stretched wide, pulled to their limits. 'Something else we invented,' Bass said with an evil grin.

'We're goin' to drag you around this godforsaken land until we reach the spot,' Korne menaced. 'Let's hope you're healthy enough to let us know where that is. OK Mo, let's ride.'

At first, the two horses moved in unison, slowly with Wesley between them, walking to keep up. Then the pace quickened and Wesley ran, his feet tripping, his breath rasping and thick. When the gravel strip narrowed, Korne and Parker stopped their mounts, wheeled and rode back at him. Wesley tried to keep to his feet, but after half-a-dozen steps he went down, and tortures shot through his body.

His chest hit the ground, pain and fear tearing at his brain. He was bumped and dragged, his shirt, then his chest ripped and torn by the gravel. Then it stopped and he lay with the back of his head on the ground, his tortured chest rising and falling, every movement bringing agony. He glared up at the squat figure of Mose Parker, heard Korne's voice, but the words made no sense.

Wesley swallowed painfully. 'You don't know much about human nature, do you, Korne?' he gasped out. 'If I wasn't going to tell you before, I'm damned if I am now. You really are a cretin.'

The horses wheeled again, dragging his body in a

circle before starting off again. He dragged his chest clear of the ground by drawing his arms into his body, the gravel now tearing at his thighs for a few moments before he collapsed down again.

His mind was fighting against a closing shroud of oblivion, darkening with every successive moment, when the sharp whack of sound broke through. He thought it was something inside his head that had snapped, but then the movement of the ground against his tortured body stopped, and he heard a yell from Korne.

He twisted to his side, saw Korne lying on the ground nursing his left arm and cursing. Parker slipped awkwardly from his saddle, shouting unintelligibly and looking across to the other side of the creek. The ground rose sharply, but there was no barren rock. There was timber and brush, and the sharp report had come from a concealed rifle higher up on the slope.

The rifle barked again and the next moment, Wesley felt a violent tug on his arms and he was being dragged once more. Both horses were frightened and out of control, but they were almost at the edge of the dry gravel, with little choice but to race into the creek shallows.

The horses slackened as the water deepened, and the ice-cold water acted fiercely on Wesley's numbed brain. The horses faltered on, finally coming to a trembling halt around a crook in the narrow valley. Wesley pushed himself to his knees, for a few moments listened to the muffled crack of rifle shots and the booms of pistols.

'It's the goddamn Styx,' he spluttered, rubbing water from his eyes and ears. Slowly he got to his feet standing thigh deep in the water. The horses were standing still, but their ears flicked back and forth in fearful uncertainty. Their eyes rolled, muscles and sinews bunched ready to bolt again. Aware that a quick movement might set them on the move again, Wesley mumbled some soothing sounds, issued soft curses as he worked slowly on one noosed arm.

When he had freed his right arm from the wet rope, the iron-grey coloured horse turned and moved away, back towards the bank. The other wanted to follow, and Wesley hauled in the rope with his free hand and slipped the noose. But he kept a tight hold, letting himself be dragged until they too cleared the water.

'That's right. I'm the good guy and you're coming with me.' He patted the grey's neck, muttering continuously, led it across to the bank on the opposite side. Part way up the slope, he tethered it to the branch of a gnarled oak and pulled the carbine from its saddle-scabbard.

He looked down at the streaked rawness of his chest. Small bits of gravel pitted his flesh and he grimaced, prising one or two out with his fingernails. Every movement caused him spiky pain, but the reviving effect of the icy water and to a greater extent, being free, had left him in a more confident frame of mind.

From around the bend in the creek, the shooting was continuing. 'What the hell's going on back there?' he said quietly, speculating on the identity of the unseen rifleman. *Thanks anyway. Right now, I guess thine enemy's my friend,* he thought, and grinned doubtingly.

Thick brush impeded him as he made his way in the direction of the shooting, but he moved up the rise until he reached the trees above. He was able to pinpoint the sharp bark of the rifle, and crouching low, he weaved his way towards the shooting.

Intending to approach the rifleman from behind, he stayed well back from the edge of the slope. He didn't want to risk being shot at mistakenly by the man who had saved him. He saw a movement in the trees to his left, stopped and waited until he saw that it was a lone horse stomping a foreleg. He walked on slowly, the sharp report of the rifle getting closer, louder in his ears.

Moments later, Wesley saw the man. He was facing away from him, crouched low, sighting along his gun barrel. When the rifleman sent another shot whipping down into the valley, Wesley moved a few steps closer. In the brief silence that followed, he snapped a twig underfoot and the darkly bearded face of Grover Garve turned towards him.

14

Wesley lifted the barrel of the carbine, his finger tight on the trigger. 'Take it easy, Sheriff,' he warned. 'I'm nervous enough. You wouldn't want to jigger me any more.'

A sudden barrage of gunfire crashed through the brush and low branches. It broke the tension and Garve ducked. 'Get yourself down,' he called out. 'It's them you got to worry about, not me.'

The tone of urgent and apparent camaraderie in Garve's words surprised Wesley. It was the last thing he expected to hear from the man who'd been responsible for putting him in jail for those five long years. But now the same man had just saved him from being skinned alive. Almost certainly saved his life.

'OK Garve. Right now you've got the high ground, and in more ways than one. But I'm carrying memories,' Wesley answered, without any shared feeling of unity.

Garve grunted out a suitable response, turned his back and commenced firing. The three men in the valley were out of sight, but a wreath of low, curling gunsmoke told of where one of them was taking cover.

'I'll take whoever's behind that boulder to the right,' Wesley said crouching alongside Garve.

'Yeah. Goddamn fish in a goddamn barrel, now,' Garve said readily, bringing his rifle up. 'I don't have to keep switchin' from one to the other. They come out each time I fire a shot . . . reckon I ain't got time to get off a second shot. But you can, Wes. You understand?'

Wesley nodded and readied himself with a careful aim. Garve's gun barked and the bullet chipped a scar in the rock opposite. At almost the same instant as Garve was uttering a triumphant snort, the man behind the boulder jerked up. He slammed a shot towards the small puff of gunsmoke he'd seen from Garve's position. But Mose Parker was unaware of Wesley's presence, and he gasped in pain, knowing it was the last mistake he'd ever make, before dropping lifeless to the ground.

'It was the risk you ran,' Wesley rasped quietly, levering another shell into the carbine's chamber.

A string of yelled curses were followed by random blasts from sixguns below. The two men were firing with unsighted fury, throwing wild, speculative shots from the rocks that sheltered them.

'Huh, bullets are a long ways off, feller,' Garve returned. 'We could almost catch 'em from this distance.' He glanced towards Wesley. 'Haven't they got rifles?' he asked.

Wesley shrugged. 'I've got one of them. I guess when they mete out their sort of killing, they're usually up close.'

Wesley and Garve flung themselves back down into cover as bullets continued to tear through the brush above their heads. Then the gunshots suddenly stopped and there was no more sound.

'Must be a limit to how much ammo they're carryin',' Garve suggested. 'Even gunnies got to run out, sometime.'

Cautiously, Wesley raised his head. He saw Bass moving to the underhang, then out of sight. He watched and waited, but his next sighting of the big half-breed was some distance upstream, still hugging the shadowed rocks.

'They've gone,' he muttered. 'There were two horses further up, and mine was one of them. I've got one of their's down below. I reckon they'll try to get up here, so we'd best get down there.'

'Yeah. Just as long as they give us a chance to do what we got to do, huh?'

Wesley turned and looked directly at Garve. 'What's brought you out here, Garve? Like right now.

115

Did you know I was in Calido Run?'

Garve's bearded face manufactured an ingratiating grin. 'Damnit, Wes. Ain't it enough that I was around?' he asked. 'They weren't escortin' you to a hoe-down, you know. They were draggin' you to death until I started in. Don't cut that out o' the herd.'

'I'm not cutting anything out. Specially not the five years of my life I spent in Yuma. That was courtesy of you,' Wesley said levelly.

'Now listen here, Wes—' Garve began.

'You trailed me here with the idea of jumping me if and when I found that gold. That's what you're doing,' Wesley interrupted.

Garve remained silent for some moments while he thought, his eyes consciously avoiding Wesley. 'Yeah, sure I trailed you here,' he admitted with a shrug of his heavy shoulders. 'But I figured on goin' shares with you. Wouldn't anyone have done the same thing?' He turned to face Wesley, inching his chin a bit closer. 'Christ, Wesley, I've been trailin' that gold for years on an' off. I'm not that much different to your ol' man.'

'Except what he found didn't belong to someone else.'

Garve's eyes narrowed, and the affable mask slipped for an instant. 'You're gettin' me mixed up with Farley Korne an' his cut-throats,' he said. 'They don't aim to play dibs for a quarter share. Hell, if you'd only listened to me five years ago, we'd both have been rich now.'

'You had me tossed in jail.'

'No, Wesley, you did that yourself. I made you an offer, an' you refused. I would've risked goin' to jail by oversteppin' my duty. But I figured that if you weren't goin' to trust me, I'd be a damned fool to stick my neck out. That's why you went to jail. No other reason.'

Wesley gave a short laugh. 'You've sure got a way of looking at things, Garve. Almost reasonable.' For Wesley, Garve was a liar and a crook. But now they were thrown together, and adversity made strange bedfellows. 'We're up against Korne and that fiendish pet killer of his. So if we come out of this, and the claim's valuable enough, I might consider some sort of dividend,' he offered. 'But make a mistake, and you join them. Understand?'

'Sure, Wes,' Garve accepted eagerly. 'I ain't for dyin' greedy.'

'You and me both. But we've still got to get out of this goddamn gulch. Seems to me, we wait here and hope they come this way to ambush them, or we take a chance by going down below.'

Garve grinned. 'We don't have to do either. I've poked in every nook an' cranny of Calido Gulch, an' there's another way out. Once above the trees, we can get high an' clear into the mountains . . . make a long detour to the north. We won't even need to go back to town. What do you think?' he said.

Wesley remembered the far end of this southern arm, the slope away to the north, the distant mountains, and he nodded in agreement. It suited him because Mariposa was always going to be his destination. And now Amy Chard was set in his thoughts and feelings. It wouldn't be an easy journey. Farley Korne and Jack Bass constituted an arm's-length danger, whereas the shifty, gold-hungry Garve presented a much closer one. Wesley grinned, realizing that any trouble would have to come after he'd found the gold, not *before*. And that was on top of whether Garve was actually a killer or not.

There would be long summer twilights in which to go about digging, and Wesley wanted to get started. He stood up and looked across the valley. 'It's a good day for vultures,' he muttered wryly, seeing the body of Mose Parker laying sprawled below him. Certain that Korne and Bass weren't going to pull out with nothing in their pokes, he pondered on their next move. He was tempted to stick to the higher ground, make the chance to ambush them. But that would mean waiting around until after first dark.

'I've got some gear with my horse,' he said at length. 'There ain't much, but it's mine, bought and paid for. So, first off, we'll move down.'

Garve shook his head and grinned. 'No need. I always carry a spare set o' duds,' he said. He nodded at Wesley's blood-spattered chest. 'That looks worse than it is, but it needs cleanin' up. I tell you, Wes, you'd be in one hell of a mess if I hadn't turned up.'

'Yeah, so you keep saying,' Wesley replied. 'Let's hope you get well rewarded for it.'

Wesley followed Garve to where he'd seen the tethered horse. There was a chunky saddle roll behind the cantle, and Garve opened it up. There was a small shovel, a short-handled pick, some tins of food, spare trousers and a wool shirt. Wesley carefully removed his own shredded remnant of a shirt and covered his sore chest with the clean one. His trousers and boots were wet, but there was no point in changing them as he'd soon be back in shallow water.

15

As yet there was neither sight nor sound of Farley Korne and the big Apache half-breed, and uncertainty niggled at Wesley's stretched nerves. If he and Garve went down to the creek, and if the two men came back and spotted them, their positions would be reversed. The advantage would then be with Korne and Bass. Sometimes, compromise was the safest contingency plan Wesley decided.

'I think we'll wait here a bit longer,' he said.

'Why? We've got to move, an' quick,' Garve replied, impatient.

Taking Garve's advice didn't come naturally or easy to Wesley. 'If they don't come up here in the next half hour, we'll know they got good reason to hang around. Maybe they reckon the gold is where they spotted me,' he ventured, adding a sour smile.

'You've found it then?' Garve's eyes blazed greedily

'You've actually seen where the gold is?'

'I didn't say that,' Wes corrected. 'Anyway, we're waiting here awhile. Tie your horse in.'

Five long minutes later, Wesley's body stiffened when he picked up the sound of hoofs coming from the north. He cursed, and his fingers tightened around the stock of his carbine.

The riders were well over towards the rising hills, but they were coming in at a long angle to get down the slope into the valley.

'Now we move,' Wesley snapped. 'We'll catch them on the slope.' He led the way at a run, moving all the time closer to the rising ground. Now and again he caught sight of the two riders as they wound in and out of the trees and high brush. They were heading to a point at the top of the slope, about fifty yards ahead of him. He crouched as he moved forward, heard Garve's quick, eager breaths, close behind him. Then with a shock, Garve's rifle exploded.

Wesley swung around. 'You goddamn fool. . .,' he started.

But Garve was lying on the ground. In his feverish anxiety to get within range of the two riders, the man had stumbled and fallen. The gunshot had been unintentional, but the damage was done.

Bass's voice yelled out and Garve scrambled to his feet, working a cartridge into the breech as two Colts blasted out in unison. Korne and Bass were shooting

121

from their saddles, but their pace was slowed, as they worked towards the crown of the slope. The range was too long for a Colt, and the bullets were wide as Garve's rifle exploded again.

Korne swung his horse on a different track. Then he dragged on his reins, swung down from the saddle and dragged his rifle from its scabbard. He went down out of sight behind brush, and a moment later his rifle spat viciously from cover.

'Don't go trying to catch those bullets. I think that's a Winchester he's using,' Wesley called out to Garve as he made a run for the cover of the bole of an oak. He quickly took aim and squeezed off a shot. But Bass had seen him and turned his horse at the moment Wesley fired. Wesley gasped when the animal faltered, as it took the bullet in its neck. He continued cursing as the horse's forelegs buckled and it went down in a headlong somersault. Bass was thrown clear and Wesley ran from cover.

'Goddamn redskin,' he yelled in unrestrained, angry accusation.

That the half-breed was still alive and probably unhurt was obvious seconds later, when the man's gun blasted through the brush. Wesley sent a bullet into the rising curl of gunsmoke, levered another shell and stood very still, waiting silently.

Bass's Colt blasted again, but this time, thirty feet from where he'd last fired. Wesley hunkered down, triggered off another shot as a bullet snatched bark from the oak, inches above his head. Under another hail of bullets, he flattened himself against the ground. 'So much for running out of ammo,' he muttered, taking deep breaths and trying to make sense of the predicament. To his left, he could hear Garve's rifle splitting the air with its sharp brittle explosions, and from ahead, Korne's sixgun was booming.

Wesley inched away from the tree, started to move closer to the high brush which was being used by Bass to such good effect. He had a sudden glimpse of the man who, in an effort to get closer, darted across a break in the undergrowth. Wesley realized that in losing his horse, Bass had little option other than to pick up the fight. He couldn't make a run for it, even if he wanted to, and he wasn't going to surrender.

Wesley was deeper in the brush now. He crawled warily forward, towards where he'd seen Bass running. But even his cautious movements were enough to bring two more bullets ripping through the foliage beside him. He lay still, his heart thudding against the ground. He was suddenly aware then of the complete and utter silence around him. Neither Garven or Korne's guns were sounding, and a pang of doubt surged through him. Was Garve dead, or had he won out against the professional gunman? Or had he made a deal, part of an elaborate and dangerous hoax to get Wesley killed? The latter seemed unlikely, making it all the more vital for him to settle with Jack Bass.

He lay still as a corpse, half closing his eyes in an effort to highlight any sound. The silence was unnerving, and he watched, mesmerized, as a ground beetle began a lazy, inquisitive walk up on to the back of his hand. The merest whisper of sound came over on his right, and the undergrowth started to shake and shimmer. The beetle turned and walked back to the ground. *Yeah, must be a safer place somewhere,* Wesley thought as he re-positioned himself.

The big half-breed had the advantage of his Colt at close quarters. But Wesley reckoned he had an edge. He moved his hands to tilt the gun up from the ground, angled it in the right direction, held it and waited. Another sound of movement drifted in, and Wesley squeezed the trigger. He heard a low grunt, the thrashing of foliage from just ahead and to his right. He levered the carbine's action and fired again.

A moment later, he slowly and shakily got to his feet. He saw the cracked and broken brush where Bass had lain, moved forward until he was staring down at his spread-eagled body.

'You don't even know if it's worth dying for,' he said after a long moment of reflection. Then a sound from behind had him turning quickly, swinging up the barrel of the carbine.

'OK Wes?' It was Garve's voice and not an altogether unwelcome sound.

The man was moving towards him, his rifle pointing directly at Bass. 'Looks like he finally made his happy huntin' ground, eh Wes?' Garve said scornfully. 'Don't reckon he contributed much to society.'

'Yeah, not like you eh?' Wesley returned. 'What happened to Korne?'

'I sent him off with his tail between his legs.' Garve's smirk became a sneer. 'Like most goddamn pack leaders, he looked to his own hide first. He took the horse, left the Indian to shoot it out while he got clear.'

'That's how you stay goddamn pack leader.' The sound of weariness was clear in Wesley's voice. 'So you know which way he went?'

'Yeah. Down the slope an' into the valley towards the gulch. But the way he was forkin' that mount, he'll be damn lucky not to break either o' their necks, before he gets back to where the two creeks connect.'

'He won't. Trust me,' Wesley said, walking forward. He leaned down and grasped the shoulder of Bass, turned him so that his dark, scarred face looked to the sky. 'You should have stayed on the Reservation,' he added. 'And there was me thinking you Apaches were smart.'

'We are. But you weren't meant to be,' Bass hissed painfully before his eyes closed.

'OK, go get your horse,' Wesley snapped out at Garve. 'I'll go down the slope and find mine. He bent and picked up Bass's Colt, shoved it peevishly into his holster.

Garve's dark eyes glinted briefly with anger. But when Wesley looked at him to get going, his face was returning its look of camaraderie.

Wesley was down the slope, sitting in his saddle when Garve came riding alongside. 'We're heading back up the creek. Follow me,' he said, leading the way. He had no concern about Garve riding behind, reminding himself that the man would only resort to treachery after the gold had been revealed. So, fully armed, and with the odds more even again, Wesley felt curiously at one with the world.

16

Grover Garve looked across the shallow lake, below the falling rope of water. 'Is this it? Goddamnit, is this the place?' His voice was thickening, almost breaking with excitement. 'Where, Wes, where? Over the other side? That goddamn waterfall should've been the marker. Have you started diggin' yet?'

'Shut it for a minute,' Wesley commanded testily.

Garve's babbling was like that of a crazy man. But back in Calido Run, Armstrong Dove had told Wesley that it wouldn't take more than the proximity of gold to spark off the man's madness. Now, Wesley believed that an actual sighting would derange him, make him dangerous. He put his hand down and touched the lariat, wondered when would be the best time to get him trussed up.

Garve kicked his horse forward into the shallow water. Wesley was about to follow, but reined in sharply at the carried sound of hoofs clipping on the hard rock down towards the creeks.

'Stay where you are,' he called out to Garve. 'Did you hear that?' He looked down the shadowed valley, but the twists in the walls prevented a view of the approaching riders. Not wanting to be caught off guard again, he swung his horse away from the water.

Garve cursed with frustration and fear, dragging out his gun and following Wesley. 'Damn him. It's Korne,' he mouthed.

'I don't think so,' Wesley said. 'And it sounds like there's more than one horse. Let's get to that outcrop.'

Wesley and Garve urged their horses down to where a rocky buttress jutted out across part of the gulley floor. The hoofbeats sounded to be very close when a Colt suddenly blasted. The echo of the shot had scarcely died away when the leading rider appeared, swinging around the projecting rock and coming directly towards the two men.

'Looks like a goddamn kid,' Wesley exclaimed staring at the slim, young rider crouched low over the claybank filly's neck. He had no time for more than a glimpse before his attention swung to the pursuing rider. 'There's more goddamn folk out here, than comes to meet the Tucson Flyer,' he rasped.

Another shot sounded, and this time the horse ridden by the fleeing young rider slipped, lost its footing. It staggered sideways, trying to keep its feet on the shale, but ended in sprawl, tossing its rider clear as it fell.

The rider who was chasing, looked up to see Wesley and Garve ahead of him, and dragged hard on his reins.

'Goddamn you, Farley Korne,' Garve bellowed.

Korne slammed out two quick shots at the man, then swung his horse, frantically digging hard with his spurs.

'I said it was him,' Garve continued in panic, as Korne disappeared around the outcrop.

Paying no heed to the danger of a waiting gun, Wesley sent his horse into a full gallop. But Korne wasn't waiting. He was bent low in his saddle, getting every ounce of strength from his mount.

On the treacherous ground, Wesley needed both hands to hold his horse steady and he kept his Colt holstered. Korne too, wasn't attempting anything else other than the arduous and testing ride. But very quickly, Korne's horse started to flag. It was losing ground to Wesley, and it changed course, clambering up the steep slope.

Korne's intention was clear. Up on timber covered ground, he would have more than an even chance for his kill. He wanted the advantage, and the tightly wooded terrain gave him one. But the steep climb was more than his already tired horse could take, and

Wesley was now closing in rapidly. He pulled his Colt and twisted in his saddle.

Wesley wrenched on one rein, almost toppling his horse, but swerving clear of Korne's bullet. Korne fired again, and this time it was wide. Wesley steadied himself, drew his own Colt and returned fire. The gunfire fused in a common roar, but it was Wesley's carefully aimed bullet that found its mark in Korne's body.

Korne pitched sideways from the saddle, his foot trapped in the stirrup. Crazed with fear, the horse plunged up the slope, dragging Korne for fifty or sixty feet before coming to a trembling, exhausted halt.

Wesley rode up, dismounting to look down at the dirt-encrusted face of the gunman. 'Some twist of fate,' he gasped.

But Korne hadn't felt what it was like to be dragged by a horse. Wesley's bullet had hit him in his chest, too close to his heart. He was dead before his body hit the ground.

'That just about concludes any deal or business you reckon we had, Farley,' Wesley added wretchedly. 'Now we've all got five wasted years.'

Wesley released the man's foot from the iron, looped the horse's reins over his arm and remounted. Riding back, he wondered why Korne had been chasing the youngster. *Must have been something real*

*important to go risking a ride back into the chops of two
unfriendly guns,* he reckoned.

He rounded the rocky outcrop at a canter, but
there was no sign of Garve or the kid – only a sombrero laying close to the injured filly. The pair had
disappeared, and staring around him in bewilder-
ment, Wesley drew his Colt, again.

'What next?' he muttered, before raising his voice.
'Garve. Where the hell are you?'

'I'm right here, Wes.'

Wesley turned to see that Garve was standing close
to the jutting rock, his horse beside him. He wore a
hopeful grin, and was gripping the arm of the kid,
except it was Amy Chard. Released by the loss of the
sombrero, the girl's raven black hair cascaded on to
her shoulders.

Wesley cursed silently and with surprise, staring at
the girl he'd imagined was waiting for him back in
Mariposa. She was dressed in a pair of jeans and a
shirt, and despite her drawn pallor, she looked more
attractive than she had in the skimpy yellow dress
she'd been wearing when he'd first met her.

'Is there anyone in the whole of New Mexico who's
not after my pa's gold?' he said wryly. 'Amy, I thought
we. . . .' he continued, but stopped short when he
saw her hands tied behind her back, and the trailing
rope. 'What the hell are you doing?' he snarled at
Garve. 'Cut that goddamn rope away from her.' With

131

rising excitement, he climbed down from his saddle, turned to find himself looking into the barrel of Garve's Colt.

'Get rid o' them guns, son. . .both of 'em,' Garve said in a thin, menacing voice. 'An' be very careful. I'm not so bad as to miss you from here.'

17

Wesley stood stock still as he looked from the bearded snarl of Garve, to Amy's dirt-grimed face. Her big, brown eyes looked frightened, and his stomach twisted with anxiety.

'I'm sorry, Wes,' Amy said. 'I should have waited for you back in Mariposa. It was what you said to do, I know. I didn't understand and got to wondering about what you'd told me. I wanted to help. When I got to Calido Run, everyone was talking about the gold . . . your pa's gold. I couldn't just wait to see if you'd come back. My luck's never been that good.'

'I said I would, Amy,' Wesley returned. 'You came all the way out here alone?'

'No, I had a guide. This man here offered, but I didn't trust him.'

Wesley balled his fists, shot an objectionable glance at Garve.

'One of the girls in the saloon who used to work with me in Mariposa, told me of someone,' Amy continued. 'He was a good old feller called Levi Norton, and they killed him, Wesley.'

'Who's *they*?'

'Someone called Beaver John. He wasn't exactly my sort either. But it was Garve that shot Levi.'

Wesley turned back to Garve. 'Killing Levi Norton took some sand, Garve. I wonder if it's all run out for you?'

Garve shifted his Colt, pressed the barrel into Amy's side with a force that made her wince. 'There's enough for me to enjoy this pretty little creature,' he rasped back. 'Now toss them guns away if you don't want to see me try. I mean it, son. My good nature's failing with the light.'

Slowly, carefully, Wesley hefted his Colt and sent it splashing in to the creek. Then he took the rifle from its scabbard and did the same.

'That's good,' Garve said. 'Keep actin' agreeable like that, an' no harm'll come to you or the girl.'

Wesley wanted time to think, time to turn the tables. 'What are you doing chasing Amy.'

'Farley Korne an' his gorillas took us by surprise in the gulch. We intended comin' back, but meantime they found the cave where we'd put her for safe keepin'. Beaver John was backshot.'

'Sometimes, death's a real gift, whichever way it

comes,' Wesley rasped.

'You got a smart tongue on you, Wes. You an' the girl. But it won't do you much good.' The fix in Garve's eyes dropped down to Amy, and he grinned maliciously. 'Yeah, she got away from 'em all right, an' now I'm a jump ahead 'cause of it. I had me a gain back there in the gulch, an' that's why I'm chasin'. She's my trump card, an' I want her back.'

Wesley's heart-rate leapt. Anger was taking over from cautious thinking. Other than his ma and pa, there'd never been any person he'd have killed for. But now he possessed the emotion of a man who cared little for his own life, in favour of Amy Chard.

The thought overwhelmed him and he leapt forward. Garve staggered backwards, dragging Amy with him, but with a shocked cry she fell to the ground. Garve's gun roared out and a bullet whammed past Wesley's ear.

'Don't be so stupid. Do you both wanna die?' Garve yelled. He levelled his Colt to within a few feet of the helpless Amy. 'You don't help me out, Wes, I'll shoot her right foot, then her left. She won't be such a catch, then eh?'

Knowing he wasn't going to be much good dead, Wesley didn't retreat. He was almost within an arm's length of Garve, and if it hadn't been for Amy he would have taken his chance of a bullet. But he heard the ominous click of the hammer as Garve thumbed it back, needing only the slightest movement to maim Amy.

'Just get back,' Garve warned. 'You want to have a dump cripple on your hands?'

Wesley backed off slowly, but his eyes remained hostile.

Beneath his dark whiskers, Garve's face was ashen, beaded with sweat. He'd had a scare at the sight of Wesley's uncontainable anger. It meant beware, take heed. 'I might just shoot for the hell of it, if you surprise me again,' he said thickly, as he eased back the Colt's hammer.

'I won't. You've made your point,' Wesley replied, his breathing laboured. 'You want the gold, and you figure on using Amy to bargain with. In your position, I guess I'd do the same.'

'There you go. We really ain't so different,' Garve mocked.

Wesley thought his back-down would settle Garve, hopefully give him the time he needed to re-think the situation. 'There's no need to bargain any more, but you'll let Amy go. Let her ride back to Calido Run,' he offered in consideration of his next move.

'When I see that yellow stuff, you can both go to kingdom come, for all I care.'

'Yeah, well forgive me if I don't go all jiggy on that,' Wesley retorted. 'I want her to go now.'

'What *you* want don't amount to a hill o' beans,

136

son,' Garve said, grinning sneerily. 'Kiss my trump card into the pot? You must think I'm a rare sort o' dumb cluck.'

Wesley shook his head, despairingly. 'No. I'm just giving you my word.'

'That's *your* word. What's to stop her runnin' to the law, once she's safely back in town? Them sendin' out a goddamn posse?'

'I've already shown you where the gold is. What more do you want, Garve?' Wesley asked, keeping a leash on his anger. 'And Amy won't speak to anyone about all this, if I ask her not to.'

'Hah. She'd agree to most anythin' to get clear, an' so would you,' Garve snorted. 'As for the gold, you only said you reckoned its whereabouts.'

'I said I'd share it with you.' Wesley was now getting more anxious. 'I've got more than one reason for loathing you, Garve, and you know it. But you were there when Korne was dragging the life from me. So, you take the gold if you want. Take it all. I'm prepared to square it.'

Garve's eyes narrowed cunningly. 'I've seen men change mighty quick when there's gold about. An' I know what they call me back in Calido Run,' he said. 'Maybe now you figure on keepin' your word. But can I take the chance?'

Looking into the scheming eyes of Garve, Wesley knew that nothing he could say now would convince the man. Garve had his standards and he applied them to everyone else. And Garve wouldn't allow himself or Amy to ride away, because there'd be no sleep or living high off the hog. Not as long as the man he'd robbed was still alive.

So Wesley had to let Garve think he was accepting the set-up. He would have to comply with what the man wanted, go along with his demands, wait or create an opportunity to jump him. It would mean one hell of a risk, but the alternative was an odds-on death wager.

'Seems to me you've no choice if you want me to recover the gold. But in return, I'm taking a chance on you keeping your word.' Wesley's proposition was difficult, and he hoped his face didn't betray any deceit.

Garve grinned his approval. 'It's a deal,' he said, his voice more open, almost friendly. 'You finger that gold, Wes, an' you're both free to go.' He gestured ahead of him. 'We'll walk back, an' you can lead both your horses. I'll be right behind you with the girl.'

18

It was well into first dark by the time they approached the waterfall, and obvious to all, it wouldn't be possible to start the search for the lode until the following morning.

Garve's eyes glittered in the falling light. 'An' you're certain this is the place?' he asked in greedy anticipation.

'I'm hoping,' Wesley answered back. 'Almost as much as you are.'

Garve was irritated and impatient. He was anxious to confirm the find, but he knew the danger of starting a search when it would soon be night. 'We'll camp on this side . . . start first thing,' he growled reluctantly. He looked from Wesley to Amy, then grunted to himself. 'It ain't goin' to be too comfortable wearin' a rope, not after what you've been through,' he said. 'But you ain't goin' to die 'cause of it. If you do try anythin', the girl gets them feet I mentioned earlier. That should keep your mind on track.'

Wesley nodded with what looked like resignation. But he was wound tight, thinking the most effective time to make a move on Garve would be straight after saying he wouldn't do any such thing. He watched edgily as Garve cut a length from the tail of rope that held Amy.

Garve started towards him, but came up short and gave a thin smile. 'I can feel your thinkin', Wes,' he said shrewdly. 'I guessed it was goin' to be now, or in them early black hours.' He went back to Amy and untied her bound wrists. 'So you'll be doin' it for me,' he said, handing Amy the end of the lariat. 'I don't suppose you normally use a rope to keep a feller down.'

He stood back and levelled his Colt on Amy, watching closely as she fastened Wesley's hands behind his back. When she'd finished, he stepped in and inspected the knots. 'Good. Now bring the rest o' the rope down an' do the same to his ankles,' he commanded.

'That'll do,' he approved a minute later. 'Huh, I've known fellers who'd pay a full dollar to have that done to 'em.'

'I'd sit down before you fall down,' he then advised Wesley, failing to notice the emotional heave of the bound man's chest, as he went about re-tying

140

Amy's wrists. 'I guess you've earned supper,' he told her. 'Now get over against that rock, an' make yourself comfy.'

When Garve had loosely roped Amy's ankles, he prowled around for dried sticks and branches to make a camp fire. 'You know what we use to get our fires started?' he said, leering towards Amy. 'We pluck them warm, downy bits o' fluff from our paunch buttons.' He chuckled offensively, but went across to his horse and pulled his saddle roll. He first took out some tools, then a small coffee-pot, then a packet of dried pork.

With water from the creek, he brewed coffee. He sipped it quick and scalding hot, before holding the tin mug up to Amy's lips. 'It ain't Arbuckle's, but then we ain't fine dinin' are we?' he sneered. He pulled out a few scraps of the jerk meat, and offered it around. Amy and Wesley shook their heads and he smiled indifferently, hunkering down half-way between them. 'I figure we shouldn't catch any more trouble from anyone now, Wes,' he suggested. 'It's a shame about ol' Beaver, but jeez the air's sure more fragrant without him. He was a fair partner, but you know what they say about too many fingers spoilin' the pie. Anyways, you can handle the work he would've done, eh Wes?'

'All I want to do now, is get clear of you and this goddamn place,' Wesley said.

141

'You're just too good for this life, Wes. Hah, you couldn't have said the same for Farley Korne an' his pack, though. I reckon Calido Run owes me somethin' for riddin' the town o' those lawless gunslingers,' he added righteously.

'Yeah, that's right. Maybe they'll give you your job back . . . stick you with a new shiny badge.'

'Like I said, Wes. You got a smart mouth on you.' Garve chuckled deeply, heaved his big shoulders, and settled back with his rifle and Colt.

After an interminable half hour, Wesley slowly raised his head. He had waited until Garve's breathing became slow and regular, before inching forward. He dug his heels into the ground, dragged his body forward, before starting a tentative, wary roll towards Amy.

Garve rose to his feet, strode forward and stood with the toes of his boots pushing hard against Wesley's body. 'As someone who can't be trusted, you'd run me pretty close,' he grated.

Wesley groaned inwardly when Garve drew a foot back, as though to kick him in the ribs. But Garve changed his mind. He pushed his Colt back into its holster, bending to grip Wesley under his arms. 'Don't try that again,' he said, dragging him back against the rock. 'I need your shovel skills.'

Wesley closed his eyes. He laid very still with his mind working away on how to keep stringing Garve along, how to get the better of him. He knew the longer he hung out, the longer he and Amy would live. But in itself that didn't mean much, and only until the gold showed itself. Furthermore, if he misjudged Garve's patience, he'd most likely get shot dead out of anger and frustration.

Eventually, physical and mental exhaustion overcame Wesley. Through the night he was disturbed by the pain in his back and injured chest, but in the early hours, deep sleep grabbed him for an hour or so.

19

'Come on wake up. We got worms to catch,' Garve growled as he shook Wesley by the shoulder.

Wesley spat drily and cursed, slowly opened his eyes to sky through which the pale light of dawn was spreading.

There was a fire crackling and the aroma of brewing coffee wafted strongly. For the briefest moment he thought things weren't all that bad. He rubbed his eyes and looked across at Amy who was sitting with her back to the rock. He was certain he should feel guilty or sorry, and when she gave him a frail smile, he knew it must have showed in his face.

'There's coffee for later, but no grub,' Garve said. 'Times like this, you miss a partner like Beaver John. He'd have found us some sort o' meat.'

'And I'm no good to you with dead muscle. Untie me,' Wesley said.

'Yeah. But any sign o' last night's antics an' the girl won't be thankin' you,' Garve warned. He unfastened the rope around Wesley's ankles and released his wrists. When the last knot was loosened, he jabbed his Colt into Wesley's back. 'Just picture her sittin' in a bath chair,' he threatened, as Wesley rubbed feeling back into his arms and shoulders.

'Are you going to free her hands?' Wesley demanded.

'No need,' Garve replied. 'Them loose loops ain't worryin' her none. Besides, I ain't havin' another pair o' hands against me, even if they've never done anythin' more than slap on face paint.'

After untying her ankles, Garve helped Amy to her feet and led her to one of the horses. He gave her a leg up into the saddle, then gestured to one of the other two horses. 'Let's not waste any more time,' he said. 'Get yourself mounted. 'A minute or so later, riding behind Amy, he told Wesley to take the lead, followed him out into the lagoon.

Wesley walked his horse across to the expanse of flat rock on the far side, dismounted and waited for Garve and Amy to ride up.

'Tether the horses. You got enough rope to manage.' Garve sniggered his instruction at Amy. 'An' you can put the shovel to work,' he told Wesley.

Seeing the avaricious glint in Garve's eyes, Wesley again wondered how long it would be before he had another chance to overcome him. Someone in the grip of gold fever was as helpless and sick as someone in any other sort of fever. At the first show of gold, Garve would almost certainly drop his guard. It would be the split second Wesley needed, but it wouldn't be just yet.

Keeping a close eye on Amy, Garve freed the shovel from its tie-string, and tossed it to Wesley. Wesley gripped it, and returned a hostile stare.

Garve's teeth showed from a lean grin as he took hold of Amy's arm. 'Don't go gettin' any more fresh ideas, Wes,' he warned. 'From this distance, a poor gun's goin' to beat a good shovel, any goddamn day o' the week.'

Wesley worked his jaw, gave Amy an imperceptible nod.

'I just want what I've been waitin' for all these years. Now, get out there an' start diggin',' Garve continued.

Wesley moved down from the flat rock and into the shallow water, cast a shrewd eye towards the line of turtle shaped rocks that rose darkly through the water. The water level didn't reach as high as his knees so close to the bank, and there were little turbulent eddies where the waterfall met the surface of the creek. A series of ripples pulsed out to the deeper water, but beyond the bubbling disturbance the water was crystal clear, and he could see polished

146

bed-stones. Providing there was a solid rock bottom lower down, it looked like an ideal reserve for any heavy metal washed from higher up. He drove in the shovel, bringing it up with a small pile of the glistening water-washed stones. He carried the small load across to the dry rock and tipped them from the curved blade of the shovel.

Garve wiped the sole of his boot across the pile, but he wasn't expecting any colour to show yet. He shook his head calculatingly, indicated that Wesley return to the water.

Wesley heeled the shovel down again, working methodically, shifting the stones from what he could see now was a natural rock-bound basin. But inexorably, a fervour started to assail him. It was the irrepressible desire to glimpse the precious metal which his father had discovered, the formation of turtle-shaped stones, proclaiming it to be the imaginary Tortola Rocks. Wesley imagined the long waterfall becoming a torrent in the wet season, gouging out the gold from the bed, tossing it over the rocks to its final resting place in the surrounding rocks.

He worked doggedly under the climbing sun. The heat spread, scorched his bent back, dredging sweat from his body. But his legs and feet were chilled, his boots were sodden weights in the ice-cold mountain water, and he fully understood why his father had returned to Calido Run with only a couple of nuggets. The old man had dug deep to test the likely cache, and then with ingrained caution, had returned the stones to cover the precious find.

The digging and slow trudge through the water was brutal toil. Each shovelful that Wesley removed had to be taken across and dumped on the flat, dry rock. The discard was rising, but as he dug deeper his shovel brought up smaller loads. Each time he drove the shovel into the gravel meant bending lower, so that he was closer to the water. Sweat was streaming down his face and his raw chest was stinging with its salty wetness.

Watching him impatiently, Garve started muttering curses, glaring down at the muddy tailings, running it between his fingers for any sign of colour. 'I'm beginnin' to think your ol' man found a couple of orphan nuggets, nothin' else,' he snarled thickly. 'Either that, or you ain't diggin' where you should be. If you're tryin' to be smart again, it ain't goin' to pay off. You'll just be out there one hell of a lot longer.'

Wesley straightened his aching back. 'I need something longer than this hayseed shovel,' he rasped. 'I can't get any deeper with it.'

'Your pa must have. So, shut up an' dig,' Garve bawled back at him.

Fighting against exhaustion, Wesley drove the

shovel down savagely. But the shovel blade went deeper than he had anticipated, and he went off-balance, into the water. The shovel had gone through the mud, and he had been brought to a sudden stop by the rock floor below. He straightened up spluttering, but excitement had its first nipping grip. If there was a gold bearing cache in the lagoon, he'd just reached it.

20

Wesley lifted the blade of the shovel and turned it towards Garve. There were only a few small smooth stones in it, the rest was black mud.

'Mud. More goddamn mud,' Garve yelled. His eyes were blazing with anger and frustration. 'You've been tuggin' my rope, feller. Your old man didn't get them nuggets from this hole, an' you knew it,' he charged.

Wesley scarcely heard Garve's voice. It was a blur of sound that didn't have any form or significance. He was looking down at the soupy blackness on the shovel. He lifted the shovel higher, holding it at the base of the handle while he flicked away a few stones. He bent down and lowered the shovel into the water, washing the mud clear to leave two small yellow nuggets of pure alluvial gold gleaming bright in the clean water.

150

In that moment of discovery, staring at his find with barely concealed exhilaration, Wesley found it difficult to think of anything else as Garve's bull voice got through to him.

'What the hell's goin' on?' the man yelled out. 'Is that gold you've got there?'

Wesley looked up from the nuggets, staring at Garve like a man who'd come through a long, debilitating trial.

Garve had moved down from the dry rock, into the water, his big hand stretching out. 'Throw me that.' The timbre had gone from his voice. Now he was frantic, more shrill. 'Throw me, goddamnit. Throw me what you got there.'

Wesley's drift into gold fever had come and gone, his thoughts snapping back to the nearby danger. 'It's the gold,' he said, nodding slowly. 'I've hit the rock floor.' He picked out the two nuggets, let the shovel splash down at his feet. He rolled the gold over in his palm, the sunlight glinting with the movement.

Garve was already wading his way through the shallow water. 'Give it here,' he was yelling.

Wesley responded by flicking up both nuggets. Garve's reaction was a reflex one, startled with hands all over the place, grasping at thin air.

Wesley dropped his hands to his sides. This was the chance he'd been waiting for; the first sight of gold that should have made Garve temporarily careless. And now, just as soon, the moment was gone, with Garve's reaction not quite what Wesley was expecting.

'You just might be goin' down after that,' he snapped. 'Huh, down to suck like a big ol' catfish. Now, grab that shovel. Start diggin' mud, an' hope there's a load more to find.'

Wesley turned away, grabbed the handle of the shovel and drove down into the water. He lifted the stones, and a few more nuggets showed in the mud when he unloaded on the flat rock. Garve stood off, before making his way back to sift for the small chunks of gold.

Again and again, Wesley moved between the sunken cache and the rock. The extent of Austen Teal's find became more and more obvious, as Garve's hands sorted out the precious yellow.

'Huh, bullets, beans, clinker. None of it beats gold.' Garve's words were garbled and rambling. 'It's a goddamn fortune. Better than anyone figured. An' all we got to do is shovel mud to get it.' He blinked, dragged his eyes from the pile to glare across at Wesley who had stopped again. 'Keep digging, damn you. Smarten up. There's more there yet,' he commanded stridently.

Wesley grunted in response. His movements had become slower in spite of Garve's frantic pressure.

There was already a fortune accumulated, but Garve was desperate for more. But Wesley was now bringing up only an occasional small nugget, and that meant that time was running out for himself and Amy. Once the digging ran dry, Garve would dispose of them both.

Wesley was very fatigued, but he made it look worse. With ponderous, sluggish movements and hoarse, panting breaths, he wanted Garve to believe that he was on the brink of collapse. He scooped up another shovelful and trudging back slowly towards the flat rock, he stumbled and almost fell. Garve, standing close, was watching him closely. With a fade in the initial excitement, the man's demeanour was cooling, becoming more speculative. With the cache clearly running dry, he had to think of a way to protect his newly acquired wealth.

21

With a timely grasp of the situation, Wesley waded forward with the loaded shovel. There was little in his manner to hint at any reserve of body strength, but in his head, a voice was yelling, 'go on, take him'. When Garve's right hand slipped down to rest on his gun-butt, Wesley looked beyond him to the pale, strained face of Amy. She too had seen the ominous movement, was taking a tentative, silent step towards Garve.

'We can leave what's left for the water gods. You've got enough,' Wesley said heavily.

Garve grinned. 'Well there's never enough, son. Just as well you ain't goin' to be around to share it,' he added. He gave a yellow-toothed smile, but there was an unstable, tell-tale quiver in his voice.

'What do you mean?' Wesley asked needlessly. 'I told you me and Amy were only interested in. . . .'

154

Wesley was still talking as he hurled the contents of the shovel blade full into Garve's face.

Garve was cursing with fury, the watery mud masking his face and half blinding him. He grabbed for his Colt, but Amy had already hurled herself at him. Garve's knees buckled as he staggered into deeper water, the gun blasting its bullet wide of its target.

'He'll kill you this time. Don't give him a chance,' were the words screaming through Wesley's head. He waded forward, swinging the shovel, slamming its blade against Garve's right arm.

Garve gasped in pain as the Colt dropped from his grasp. Wesley brought the shovel back to swing again, but Garve lunged at him, his arms grasping for a hold. The weight and momentum of Garve's body sent Wesley floundering, and he felt the shovel being wrenched from his grasp. He twisted it in a semicircle and Garve released it, but only to go spinning into the water. Immediately, Garve's free hand slammed into Wesley's chest.

Wesley grunted, drove a return punch low into Garve's middle and the big man backed away awkwardly. Then, as Wesley pursued him, Garve whipped a stubby-bladed knife from a sheath he had tucked into the back of his trousers waistband.

Wesley heard Amy's warning cry and checked his rush. He saw Garve's arm weaving side to side, the knife glittering in his hand. He twisted away, felt pain like a hot wire being drawn down his arm. It was a superficial cut, and missed its target, but at the lack of resistance, Garve lost his balance, and fell forward.

Wesley lifted his right hand, and, curling his knuckles tight, made a hard chopping drive at the base of Garve's skull. The man's dark bearded face turned to one side, his eyes glazing with pain and shock. He raised his arm, stabbing out with the knife, but Wesley was above him and gripped his wrist. With his other hand, Garve caught Wesley's temple with a flailing fist, but he dropped the knife, and Wesley staggered back a few awkward paces.

'Only us now, Garve,' he spat contemptuously. 'You're plumb out of help.'

Regaining some of his senses, using a desperate sense of survival, Garve lumbered in to take a jolting, ramrod left on his mouth. He coughed, dropped his head in agony, his breathing now shallow sobbing gasps.

Wesley swung in another left, followed it with a bone-jarring right to the side of Garve's face. Garve's knees buckled, but there was still a reserve of power in his big body. He jerked out his long arms as he fell, wrapping them around Wesley's legs to bring him down.

Wesley felt the weight of Garve against his body when he hit the water, then he felt a shoulder hit bottom, and there was water filling his mouth and nostrils. He jerked his head above water, gulped in air and tried to ward off Garve who had arched himself out of the water like an extra giant turtle. Garve plunged at him, his hands clawing for a grip on his throat.

At Garve's throttling fingers, Wesley went under water again, and the voices returned, this time hollow and distant. 'He'll drown you, Wes. There's no more chances.' It seemed that a huge waterfall was roaring in his ears and he writhed, tried to force himself up, his head from the water. He drew in his knees, feeling the impact against Garve's body as he lashed out. The grip around his throat relaxed, and he squirmed in a desperate frenzy to free himself.

Gasping for air in his starving lungs, and with the brightening sky and surrounding rocks spiralling around him, he staggered upright, dragging his feet from the thick oozy mud.

Garve was moving towards him, slowly. But he stopped suddenly, gave a little grin and started to turn away.

'Why the hell is he backing off?' The voices were yelling in Wesley's head again. 'Take the knife,' they said. 'Take the knife.' Only then did Wesley realize he was gripping Garve's knife in his fingers. By chance he'd located it when he'd been probing for hand-holds and steadiness in the cloying mud.

157

And then Garve's purpose hammered home. 'Amy, run. He's coming after you,' he yelled.

Wesley floundered after Garve as he shouted, but Amy hadn't moved. She was standing her ground beside the small pile of washed ore.

Wesley started to run as the water shallowed. He realized that Amy was using herself as bait. She couldn't defend herself, was hoping that he'd get to her before she suffered any real harm from the menacing Garve.

But Garve was savvy too. He grunted his awareness, twisting around to see where Wesley was. But Wesley was already on him, his left arm stretching out for Garve's thick neck. Wesley snapped his arm tight, dragging the man towards him and the point of the knife.

'I never had you down as a killer,' Garve managed to hiss through clenched teeth.

'I've tried my best not to be. But years ago I told you what I'd do if you ever laid a hand on me again, or called me 'son'. You forgot. I didn't.'

Garve's head dropped forward, his knees buckled and both men fell at the water's edge.

Wesley let go and regained his footing. He raised himself up, stood exhausted, watching for a moment longer. But there was no more movement from Garve, only a ribbon of darker water, coiling slowly around his lifeless body.

158

'Nothing you don't deserve. And it saves the County a hanging cost,' Wesley said quietly, turning and walking back to where Amy stood waiting for him. 'What the hell does this mean, Amy?' he asked distractedly, looking down at the cache.

'It means, if we don't want to spend the rest of our lives dodging the law, we ride back to Calido Run.'

'Yeah. Somebody told me there's a good sheriff. And then there's Mariposa. I promised an old goat at the livery there I'd come back with a good yarn. So what do we do after that?'

'Well, I don't know the full length and breadth of it, Wes. But we won't have to *go* anywhere or *do* anything we don't want.'